About the Author

Proud husband, father and grandfather; a successful businessman with a passion for researching all things WW2.

Now I Grow Oranges

Steve King

Now I Grow Oranges

Olympia Publishers
London

www.olympiapublishers.com
OLYMPIA PAPERBACK EDITION

Copyright © Steve King 2023

The right of Steve King to be identified as author of
this work has been asserted in accordance with sections 77 and 78 of
the Copyright, Designs and Patents Act 1988.

All Rights Reserved

No reproduction, copy or transmission of this publication
may be made without written permission.
No paragraph of this publication may be reproduced,
copied or transmitted save with the written permission of the publisher,
or in accordance with the provisions
of the Copyright Act 1956 (as amended).

Any person who commits any unauthorised act in relation to
this publication may be liable to criminal
prosecution and civil claims for damage.

A CIP catalogue record for this title is
available from the British Library.

ISBN: 978-1-80074-582-7

For the purpose of confidentiality and to avoid any reference that may cause offence or confusion some of the names referred to herein may have been altered slightly so as to avoid any unwanted attention or distress.

First Published in 2023

Olympia Publishers
Tallis House
2 Tallis Street
London
EC4Y 0AB

Printed in Great Britain

Dedication

My book is dedicated to all those who never had a homecoming.

Acknowledgements

Sincerest thanks to these amazing people without whose help and patience I could not have written this book. Justin Saddington, research curator, The National Army Museum. Dr Anthony Morton, D.P.S/A.R.M Curator, The Sandhurst Collection Mrs Sarah Wearne, Archivist of Abingdon School (aka Roysess school) Jonathan Holt, Archivist and Librarian, The Tank Museum. Susan Tomkins, the research team, Beaulieu. The research team, The Commonwealth War Graves Commission. Blair Southerndon, Researcher, The Rifles/Royal Green Jackets Museum. John Grehan and Martin Mace's book "Unearthing Churchill's Secret Army". The Commando Veterans Association. The Northamptonshire Yeomanry Museum. The Imperial War Museum. The National Archives. Bob Goodenough. Alan James. Nigel Bobs Sarah James, Lou Yardley, and of course, Daphne.

The Author's Introduction

June 1940, Europe had been over-run by the Nazi war machine and 330,000 service men and women of the British Expeditionary Force (B.E.F.) had just been recovered from the beaches of Dunkirk, Great Britain stood alone. Adolf Hitler had requested negotiations take place between Great Britain and Germany to cease hostilities on condition Great Britain accepts subjugate and relinquishes its Commonwealth. By and large and in principle, Parliament was prepared to accept these conditions, however, that was until Winston Churchill took to the floor to make his rousing, "We shall never surrender" speech.

Soon after, as Great Britain prepared to be invaded, Churchill tasked his friend Hugh Dalton to create a sabotage unit to operate in secret wherever Axis Forces were.

So, it was on July 22nd that Dalton reported to the War Cabinet that the Special Operations Executive had been created. Churchill replied, "And now go and set Europe ablaze."

Shrouded in secrecy, it's difficult, if not impossible, to say just how many men and women served in/with S.O.E, but approximately 140 agents are recorded as having lost their lives while doing so, some in the most barbaric of circumstances.

In many instances their missions and even their very existence, are subject to the Official Secrets Act (O.S.A). Kept under lock and key at the National Archives and subject to time embargos too. Twenty-five years was commonplace, but thirty, fifty, seventy-five and even one hundred years were also given, depending on the "delicacy" of the information held.

Mindful of the above, my book covers the exploits of one man. From childhood through schooling to conscription. From Dunkirk to Sandhurst and S.O.E. From France to North Africa, from Berlin to Buenos Aires, indeed all of the major events featured are real. The *Graff Spee* incident, the Vatican sponsored Nazi Rat Lines, atrocities like that of Oradour-sur-Glane to his one-on-one combat encounters. Training with the Commandos, parachute drops into France, fishing boats into Algeria. The events are real and well documented, however because of the O.S.A and the 100-year embargo, it is for you to decide if Sebastian Wyke is.

(To avoid any misinterpretation and to protect identity some names may have been altered slightly and any unintentional similarities are purely coincidental.)

Chapter One

Wyke is our surname, father is Charles, mother is Monique, and I'm Sebastian, Seb, to most. Born on June the 9th 1919 as an only child. My mother is French, they met when she came to stay at the Manor house just prior to WW1. It was owned by her late uncle, but when war broke out and, although her hometown of Laval, in Normandy, was miles away from the front line, her parents thought it best she stayed here until it was over. She did return immediately after the war, and took her boyfriend (father) with her; they married and then I came along.

Privileged? Yes, I suppose I was. Father is the third generation on our family farm "Windy Ridge", In all about two thousand acres of mostly pastureland on the northern slopes of the Berkshire Downs. It felt like we were in the middle of nowhere, rolling down land, chalky fields and no neighbours except for our farm hands and about four hundred heads of sheep, a small milking herd and some pigs which we keep for ourselves, oh and mother's chickens. The nearest village is East Hendred, about two miles away.

My earliest recollections are of helping mother collecting eggs for breakfast, then playing, mostly on my own around the farm, although we did have four farm cottages close by where our hands lived and there were some children there of a similar age, I was encouraged not to mix too closely with them.

Of all the adults I knew at that time, Shepherd Grace was probably the most influential. He lived in a mobile hut which was towed from location to location by our only horse. I never knew his first name, come to think of it, I doubt father knew it either, he was simply known to all as Shepherd Grace.

At five years old the scourge of all childhood came along in the form of infant school!

Each morning at eight-thirty, mother would drive me to St Wilfred's Church school in the village where there were only two classes, one for five- to seven-year-olds (mine), our teacher was Mrs Newton, and one for eight- to ten-year-olds who were taught by the headmaster, Mr Schofield.

By and large I enjoyed school, I had a thirst for knowledge, especially Geography, where I would gaze in amazement at a map of the world and all the pink bits which belonged to England, places I'd never heard of like Ceylon, Honk Kong, Nigeria, Burma and so on, I wanted to learn more about them and had made my mind up to one day visit as many as I could.

My parents were always busy people, father on the farm and mother around the house which left me ample time to spend on the land and with the shepherd. He taught me so much about country life — how to snare rabbit and how to chop its neck, paunch it, skin and cook it over a small fire. In autumn he would shoot pheasant (but I had to promise not to tell father) and pluck and draw it for his pot. Shoot the fox and carrion crow, both a threat to the sheep, especially lambs (the Crows would peck their eyes out) the alarm call of the Blackbird and the pleasing sound of the Yellow Hammer.

His hut was also home to all his worldly possessions, he had a stove for warmth and to cook on, while on the outside at the rear, was attached a chicken coup just big enough for three birds he let roam by day, but put away to roost at dusk.

He spoke to me of the stars, in particular how to locate the

North Star by a bearing from the Plough formation, saying you'll never be lost as long as you can find the North Star. He spoke of the seasons, he could tell the weather from the clouds, which plants were poisonous and which were succulent from the land he called the good Lord's Larder.

He would whittle sticks into pegs too and I remember thinking 'Why do I need to go to school? Shepherd Grace knows everything.'

But my keenness to learn (and go to school) became even more addictive after my second year, I was eight years old and I'd fallen in love!

Pamela Nicholson, she was the best-looking girl I'd ever seen, long brown curly hair, gorgeous brown eyes and a smile big enough to cheer the dullest day, I was in love.

The next three years were the best a child could wish for, loving parents, a few good friends, lots of time spent with the Shepherd — happy at school and the best girlfriend in the world, the only blot was Sam Denton, the school bully.

Samuel Denton was a nasty so and so, he came from a rough family in the village, well known for poaching, drinking and fighting. From day one he took an instant dislike to me, calling me toffee because of the "Toffee Nose" way I spoke and probably because I came from the big farm on the hill, which I can understand as his life so was much harder than mine. But his bullying came to an abrupt end when one-day in the playground he began picking on me again and hit me hard cutting my lip. Mrs Newton was attending to my wound when Schofield the Head came in, "Denton picking on you again Wyke?"

"Yes, sir."

"Well why don't you thump him back? You're bigger and stronger."

"Because I don't want to be in trouble with you for fighting, sir."

"Self-defence, my boy — self-defence." And walked away.

A week or so passed, my lip had healed and Schofield's advice was buzzing around my head to the point where I'd made up my mind next time Denton tries it on, I would thump him back — that time wasn't long coming.

Play-time and Denton came over to me, "How's your cut lip, Toffee."

"Healed nicely, Dumbo," I replied.

"What did you say?"

"You heard me."

That was it, he lunged toward me trying to grab my neck but I had a longer reach and stopped him dead by holding his lapels, he began swinging wildly, but while still holding his lapels I managed to swing him around and to the ground, as I let him go he jumped up into a boxer stance, "Come on then, Toffee." We both squared up, he took a swipe and missed but my return struck him right on the nose which instantly squashed and poured with blood, it was the first time I'd ever hit anyone and my thoughts were, 'What if he dies?' Schofield came out, "Wyke to my room!" he bellowed. 'I'm in big trouble now!' I thought.

A few moments passed and Schofield came in. "I saw what happened and I consider your actions to be self-defence, you will have no punishment — this time."

"Thank you, sir."

"I suspect Denton has well and truly been given a lesson too, so let that be an end to it."

"Yes sir, thank you sir."

At supper that evening, father said Mr Schofield had told mother what happened, before I'd uttered a word in defence father said, "Never be bullied, son, and don't be afraid of anyone except thy maker — subject closed."

Not long after, it was my birthday and father gave me a 4-10 shotgun which I would use most evenings after school on my way to see the Shepherd. Such happy times.

One of the Shepherds frequent sayings was "Nothing lasts forever" and for me that would prove to be so true.

It was summer 1930 and as we had done in previous years, Mother took me to her home in France. We crossed the channel by ferry which was great fun then took the train to Laval in the Loire where her parents had a huge milking herd. Their pastures stretched almost up to the Parc National, an amazing forest with wild boar which uncle would hunt.

On my return, and at just eleven years old, it was time for me to move up to "big" school in September and the prospect of that move wasn't too much of a problem for me as I'd most likely be going to the National School in the near-by town of Wantage — so too would Pamela!

Alas, my dream of that was shattered when father eventually told me I was going to Roysses Grammar school ten miles away in Abingdon, worse too, I was to board there during the week. No wonder they kept that a secret, how could my parents have done that to me? They had ruined my life!

There followed a few days of heavy arguing with me, often saying I would run away rather than board there but my parents were having none of it. They said, that ideally they wanted me to take over the farm one day, but that was a long way off and situations change, I may not want to. I may want to fulfil my dreams of travelling, to see the world and have new experiences, they kept saying there's more to life than farming and having the best education possible would well prepare and equip me for whatever path I choose. How right they were proven to be.

It was a Sunday afternoon in late August 1930 when mother drove me and my boarding kit to my new "prison" for the next five years. It was harvest time and Father had wished me luck earlier that morning before disappearing off to the land, the irony was one of his tractor drivers — me — would be absent by his making!

Arriving at Roysses, it was good to see other boys there about to go through the same induction, there was a brief introduction from Mr Grundy, the head, followed by tea and cakes, all very civilised and sociable to. Six o'clock came, time for parents and guardians to leave and while trying to keep my composure I bade Mother good-bye. So far so good... until we were shown to our respective dormitories, I wasn't sure what to expect, at best a room of my own? At worst, to share with another boy, imagine then my horror to find my dorm was to share with nineteen other boys!

My bed was second on the right, the first was allocated to Walter Gibson, a slightly built lad with noticeably thick glasses, he looked a proper swat! We soon struck up conversation and "Gibbo" spoke of his parents back in London, his mother was a fashion designer and his father a "Civil Servant" in the War Office, but he wouldn't expand on that. Gibbo travelled down on his own by train, although he was met at Radley station by one of the school porters. Gibbo was to prove a very good friend and not just through my time at Roysses.

To my right was Henry Thatcher, he came from Henley and apparently his father was a surgeon somewhere, he was a good sort, quiet but reliable and totally trustworthy.

So began my life at Roysses, the first year was fairly normal (if ever life could be normal at one of the finest Grammar schools in the country). Up at seven a.m., breakfast between seven-thirty and eight, then an hour to prepare for lessons which began at nine and woe be-tide any one late!

One thing I was unaware of, and I think probably Father was too, was the fact that Wednesday afternoons were reserved for clubs and activities, brilliant? No — that afternoon's academic work was to be done on Saturday mornings — a five and half day week which meant someone had to collect me a midday on Saturdays, and that didn't go down very well at home!

Year one passed pretty much without incident and I became used to seeing Pamela on Saturday afternoons and Sundays, she was changing, not only into an even more beautiful woman, but person too. No matter what was on weekends I always found time to share some moments with Shepherd Grace and often Pamela would come along as well.

Summer was too soon ending, and Roysses beckoned for my second year, it was September 1931 and school life had become much more intense. Our French lessons were great fun, at first, I didn't let on French was my second language and that I'd been speaking it with Mother for as long as I could remember, but consistently gaining top marks, I knew sooner or later I had to reveal my secret which was met with much laughter by all, including the master.

Science was becoming more and more interesting but my all-time favourite was the opportunity to join the Officer Training Corps (OTC) that, along with my sporting activities, were welcome distractions from academia.

Growing up on the farm was very much a physical existence, often with long hours and that led me to be fitter and stronger than most in my year, the upshot being I was a key member of the rugby, rowing and cricket Teams and although I thoroughly enjoyed all these sports my yearning was more and more toward the O.T.C.

As my second year came and went, I finished school with a good report, maths was something I often struggled with but luckily my good friend Gibbo would help me, he made a big difference for sure. The O.T.C. camp in summer at Tidworth Army Camp was fantastic, I won the marksman competition and was first home in the orienteering competition too, both events against boys from several other schools, so that was particularly pleasing for me (and Mr Grundy).

The summer of '32 was wonderful, I met with Pamela most days and I'm pleased to say with much approval from Mother (and to a certain extent Father too). I think Mother looked on Pamela as the daughter she never had.

With an amount of prediction and a certain amount of monotony I began my third year at Roysses which was pretty much a mirror of my previous year. Geography, History and French, reliving the misery of maths, science was okay but, as always, my favourites were what I was best at, sport and O.T.C. (now promoted to Lnc/Cpl).

Again, I played in the school rugby and cricket teams and was gaining a reputation of being unbeatable in the sculls. I was always placed as stroke in the coxed fours against the Colleges in our regular regattas on the Thames here, and we were holding our own against the likes of Lincoln, Radley, Culham, Keble and Magdalene.

With O.T.C. we held a mock battle on the downs against Radley and had another summer camp at Tidworth. Worrying though was news of what was happening in Germany, seems their new Chancellor had visions of expanding his empire?

Term ended in early July and I had another blissful summer with my beautiful Pamela which was once more cut short by the return to Roysses for the years '32/3.

This next year, much like the one that followed it (1933/34) was an enjoyable mix of learning, swatting, sports and O.T.C., Tidworth was getting better each year, as was my shooting.

The term year 1934/35 was my final year in Lower School and the anticipation of leaving Roysses to work full time on the farm and seeing Pamela each day drove me on, all was going well until the final term when my parents announced I was to stay on for another two years to obtain the Higher School Certificate.

Previous experience proved there was little point in objecting and come late August, I found myself beginning two years in the Upper School — the only consolation being I was to share a dorm with one other boy instead of nineteen, and to much delight, it was with my dear friend Gibbo. 1935/36 was pretty much full on although being in Upper School meant we were treated much more like adults. My year end results were good, even my maths had improved, but summer camps with O.T.C. were the highlights.

Summer came and went and so I began my final year, 1936/37. Gibbo and I would often have long conversations about the situation in Germany, I think with whatever his father did, he was better informed than most? Sometimes we would discuss the worsening situation in class too, especially in Geography where we would plot on a wall map of Europe Germany's annexation of its neighbours.

My final term at Roysses was one of mixed emotions and reflecting on my time I concluded for sure I'd had an exceptional education and attained all my expected certifications. At times I'd captained the rugby and cricket teams, was captain of the Rowing Club, had been promoted to Platoon Sergeant in O.T.C.

and was an unbeaten marksman. However, with the words of Shepherd Grace "Nothing lasts forever" in my mind, I said farewell to my tutors, school chums and me dear friend Gibbo. The world was waiting!

Chapter Two

War is Coming!

I remember it was Summer 1938 and I was heavily into the farming way of life, Pamela had left school two years earlier and was working in the village Post Office, everything seemed perfect except for the continuing bad news from Europe.

There was much talk of the Nazi party's persecution of the Jews, its aggressive stance toward Poland and apparently the rapid expansion of its armed forces. New battle ships and a well-equipped army of one million men, all very disturbing. Meanwhile Prime Minister Chamberlain had signed a treaty with Poland assuring them of military assistance should they ever be invaded, although such solidarity proved impotent in deterring "der Fuhrer" from invading Czechoslovakia.

Prime Minister Chamberlain had put us on a war footing and immediately announced increasing the size of the T.A. and ordering more ships and aircraft, it was not looking good.

1939 came with a plethora of European Summits and emergency meetings, the last of which appeared successful when Prime Minister Chamberlain returned from his meeting with the German Chancellor proclaiming a settlement had been agreed and there was to be, "Peace in our time." Even so the news was still dominated by events in Europe.

On September 1st the inevitable happened and Germany invaded Poland!

We were in the kitchen listening to the wireless as the PM reported to the nation that our government had demanded Germany ceased hostilities toward Poland and give an undertaking to do so by a deadline set as September 3rd, that deadline had passed and so it was that Great Britain was now at war with Germany!

Waking next morning expecting to hear guns, bombs and all sorts of other armaments I was pleasantly surprised to hear — silence. In fact, for the next few days everything seemed pretty normal, work on the farm carried on and I met with Pamela most days too, but a dose of reality came when two Nazi aircraft flew low overhead, they looked like Junkers 88s, an aircraft I was to see and fear for a very long time.

Much of the news broadcasts that autumn reported on how the British Expeditionary Force (B.E.F.) was amassing in strength over in France, although the War Office were deliberate in not revealing actual figures, mostly because our army was much inferior in size to that of the Nazi's, it was very much positive propaganda.

My dear friend Gibbo wrote telling me he had a position working as a civilian in the War Office in Whitehall, no doubt through his father's connections? I wrote back telling him of the uneasy dilemma I found myself in which was to enlist and put my O.T.C. training at Roysses to good use, that's what I wanted to do, but I had a commitment to my parents to continue on the farm, that was their wish and I owed them that. Then there was Pamela to consider, how would she react? Would she even understand me? What was I to do?

Before Gibbo had replied, I decided to take the bull by the horns and broach the subject firstly with Pamela who completely went to pieces at the thought of me going to war, it was awful to see her so upset, so much so I decided not to pursue the subject with her any more — for the moment. Next was to reveal my intentions to my parents both of whom I expected to blow their tops. Like Pamela, mother went to pieces and kept saying as a farmer I wouldn't be expected to enlist and that I hadn't thought the situation through, what about Pamela and bless her she came up with just about every excuse and reason for me not to join up.

Father however, having lost his brother in the first world war was surprisingly calm and quite logical. "Son, if you yearn that strongly to enlist and fight against fascism then you must follow that ambition, of course I don't want you to go, you might not come back, but you're old enough now to make that decision and I will respect and support you whatever the outcome."

Mother was distraught and, as with Pamela. I thought it best to change the subject — for the time being. However, my dilemma was settled two days later when I received notification to register for National Service!

Chapter Three

Conscription

Instructions were to report to Didcot station where I was to collect my rail warrant card, then board the next train to Reading. Once there I would be met by a rank from the Royal Berkshire Regiment (R.B.R). Mother took me to the station and after a quick goodbye off I went into the unknown.

Sure enough, at Reading there was corporal bellowing out, "Any one for Brock Barracks outside to the Army lorries!" All aboard and off to Brock we went.

On arrival we were shown to our billets and our allocated locker, then to the stores for our knife, fork and spoon, next stop the dining hall and my first taste of Army food. After that, the medical centre for the quickest medical possible then back to the billet for a night's sleep. 0600 and reveille woke me, a cold-water wash and shave then off to the barbers (I've seen sheep shorn better) then to the stores again for my kit. Two battle dress uniforms, two pairs of boots, respirator, rifle, bayonet, helmet and an over-coat. After taking this lot to my billet it was back to the medic centre where, once inside, we rolled up one sleeve for a jab, apparently a cocktail of "stuff" to ward off disease and infection.

The next six weeks were pretty hard going but luckily being as fit as I was the all-too-often ten-mile route marches were no problem, weapon training was reminiscent of O.C.T. at Roysses, but I didn't take kindly to square bashing and P.E at 0700 in the freezing cold in just a vest and shorts.

One big surprise was shortly after arriving at Brock I bumped into my old adversary, Sam Denton, he was billeted next door and thankfully in another unit, but whenever we met, he was very amiable.

Our six weeks of basic infantry training was at an end so we were told to look on our billet notice board to see where fate would be sending us next? Checking down the list it seemed everyone was to join the 4th Battalion of the Royal Berks Regiment, but not me, next to my name was 7th R.T.R.? Not having a clue what it meant I requested to see my R.S.M. who pretty much said, "Apparently the powers that be deem you more worthy of staying in this infantry regiment so you are off to join the Royal Tank Regiment — at Catterick." He went on to say, "There will be transport to take you to the station at 0900 tomorrow for your journey to Yorkshire!"

The first thing one notices about Catterick is the size of the place, it's vast and not a bit like Brock although day one was familiar: Identify your billet, then your bed, get your kit from the stores, evening meal, bed. Next day report for training proper.

We were given a quick introduction by the Commanding Officer, part of which he said he wanted to produce competent tank crews in less than six months! We were split into groups of fours and with no apparent preselection, our group was Wilfred Thomas, Eric Short, Sam Dempsey and myself, all being well this was our tank crew.

At the end of just twenty weeks, each of us would be expected to be competent at the four main tasks in a tank, that's to say: driver, gunner, loader/radio operator and commander, as well as maintenance. To say life there was full-on would be an understatement, our timetable being one day a week on each position and on Friday would be maintenance, communications and any other subjects.

Then came the news of events unfolding in the South Atlantic. The admiralty had reported they had been shadowing the Nazi Pocket Battleship, Graf Spee which they said had been visiting locations along the coast of Argentina?

Three Navy cruisers had pursued and engaged her, causing much damage to the point where her captain, Hans Langsdorff, decided to seek refuge in the neutral port of Montevideo, Uruguay. Once there she was given seventy-two hours to make good and off-load injured crew. At the end of her allotted time the Graf Spee let go and made for the open sea knowing the three cruisers waiting for her had been joined by a fourth. Her captain made the decision to scuttle her and to the bottom along with her secrets she went!

Three days later in a hotel room in Buenos Aires, Argentina, her captain committed suicide. I never understood why she was operating several thousand miles away from the theatre of war and what was so important about her and her cargo that her captain decided to scuttle his ship and then shoot himself? Perhaps her real purpose will be revealed one day.

By now we were approaching Christmas, but the hope of spending a few days at home was shattered when we were told all leave was cancelled.

And so our training rolled on and on, until at week ten we were each given our reviews and preliminary crew positions, Sam was to be loader, which included responsibility for all arms and ammo as well as wireless operator, Eric was to be driver, our gunner was to be Wilf and I was given the role of commander, why I don't know, except my time in O.T.C. while at school may have had some bearing.

Another ten weeks passed and our preliminary crew positions were confirmed as permanent, apparently, we were now ready to be let loose against the Nazis! Oh, I was promoted to Lance Corporal!

Needless to say, throughout my time away Pamela and I wrote incessantly to each other, that kept me up to date with life back home and also kept my parents and Pamela up to date with events happening in my life too.

Chapter Four

Dunkirk

It was early May 1940 when as the 7th R.T.R. we, being myself and my three original crew mates, gunner Wilf Thomas, driver Eric Short and loader Sam Dempsey loaded our tanks and equipment onto flatbed carriages for the train journey from Catterick to Dover, little did any of us know what lay ahead.

We arrived in France on the 12th, two days after the Nazi's invaded Holland and Belgium. Initially we were to travel to the front by rail, but there was a shortage of flatbed rail carriages so orders were to head east by road toward the rapidly advancing Germans. However, the roads were clogged with refugees going the opposite way which often reduced our pace to not much more than a walk.

On the 19th we suffered our first casualties of the war when four men of the 4th R.T.R. (our sister regiment) were killed in an air attack.

At that time, we were operating under French command, but information was sparse and so unreliable which in turn prompted us to send our own reconnaissance (recce) units out to search where the French were and to establish where the German front line was and on their return the recce officer — 2nd Lt Vaux — would report directly back to Brigade HQ. It was near St Amand on the 20th when his recce troop of the 4th R.T.R. had visual contact with advancing German armour and soon after began exchanging fire.

Outnumbered, the 4th withdrew and attempted to find the Regiments Head Quarters (R.H.Q.) but it wasn't until late that afternoon Lt Vaux arrived back and reported to Lt Col Fitzmaurice that by now hundreds of enemy tanks were approaching us at Arras and so a break-out plan was hatched code named Frank-Force.

Our ad-hoc force had a start time of 0500 hours on the 21st. Our objective was to break through the German columns, the 4th R.T.R. would be to the left along with troops of the 6th Durham Light Infantry (D.L.I.) while we (the 7th) had the 8th D.L.I on the right with supporting arms. The 4th R.T.R. had thirty-five Mk I Matildas and we had had twenty-three Mk I's and sixteen Mk II Matildas. The Mk II's had stronger armour and were better armed, but they were slow at cross country and suffered track problems. When the start time came (0500 hours) it was evident much of our planned force had not arrived, some tanks were still en-route and the D.L.I. were quite a way off still marching towards Arras.

The planned French tanks along with some infantry came and their Commander pulled alongside me, he was taking stock of the situation then suddenly bellowed to his force, "Inverser! Inverser!" (Reverse, Reverse).

Seeing him clearly about to withdraw I lost my temper and hollered over to him in my best French accent, "Pourquoi inversez-vous vos ordres, restez et combattez avec nous, c'est une opération conjointe!" (Why are you reversing? Your orders are to stay and fight with us, this is a joint operation!)

To which he replied, "Cette situation est sans espoir, nous vivrons pour nous battre un autre jour, au revoir." (This situation is hopeless, we shall live to fight another day, Goodbye.)

There then followed a very heated exchange between us at which point our Major ran over and asked for a translation. By now the French infantry in their halftracks were turning about and making off like there was no tomorrow. Seeing this, the Major said, "Tell him (the French C.O.) if he's not prepared to stand and fight for his country, why the hell should we?"

I did that, but had no reply, just a blank, almost vacant look to which Major then instructed, "Tell him to bugger off, rather a bullet in the front from Gerry than one in the back from you bunch of cowards." Naturally, I obeyed and the delicate French/Allied collaboration took another blow!

It was obvious our start time could not be achieved so it was put back to 1400 hours.

As usual the roads were choked with refugees and in an effort to bypass these some tanks took to going cross country — getting lost in the process and a wireless black-out order in place only added to the worsening confusion. We had no air support which meant there were numerous German spotter planes flying unchallenged overhead reporting back to their artillery on our position and strength (which much aided their already very accurate shelling).

It was hoped that the French contingent that pulled out may have new orders to return? They may have had so — but they never came!

The 4th R.T.R. crossed the railway line, which was their start-point, on time and their two squadrons side by side located and engaged the flank of the SS Totenkopf Division and that of the 6 Rifle Regiment of 7 Panzer Division simultaneously, however, maintaining wireless silence made communicating with the squadron almost impossible and to some extent tank commanders fought almost independently. The 4th made good progress and claimed many kills as they continued their attack.

We were late off our Start Line but made good progress. Major King and Sergeant Doyle in their Matilda Mk IIs completely destroyed two batteries of Anti — Tank guns together with two tanks and an 88mm gun. Sadly, though we took many casualties and by 1600 hours it became known the COs of both the 4th and 7th had been killed.

The D.L.I eventually arrived about 1630 and despite being exhausted after their long march fought courageously, often at close quarters.

By now, still with a wireless order in place and with no maps either there was much confusion as to where we were (and where we were going) so I decided to follow the Major as closely as possible which was just as well because as we were at speed along a field with thick hedge rows either side I saw some movement almost opposite the Major's tank, I shouted to my gunner, "Put one in there, Wilf!" Which he immediately did, bang on the location of an Anti-tank gun unit scoring a direct hit, the Majors turret swung around firstly to see what the almighty bang was to his left and then further around to see us following right up his arse!

We continued to engage the enemy as and when we could but we were getting further and further depleted to the point at around 1900 hours the Major stopped on the outskirts of a village and what was left of the 7th gathered around. A fairly democratic, albeit brief, discussion took place regarding our situation and the consensus was to continue as best we could and hope the night may bring us some much-needed re-coup time.

Next day we continued to engage with the enemy while not ever being totally sure of where we were, although we were aware the Royal Berkshire's (the biscuit boys) were in the thick of things further north. That night (22nd) with what was left of the 4th and 7th R.T.Rs along with the remaining lads of the D.L.I we made for Vimy Ridge and took cover in the woods there, using the time to make good and recover as best we could.

First light on the 23rd and we were off heading toward Carvin, but it wasn't long before we met with a column of German tanks and infantry.

As we opened fire, we had the shock of our lives to see a full French Mechanised Division arrive and join in the battle and much to our immense joy beat Gerry off, a full retreat!

That evening we camped at Carvin where a new force was formed under Major George Parkes (of our 7th R.T.R.) together with what remained of the 4th R.T.R. By now (24th) the road toward Dunkirk was something to behold, like a scene from Armageddon, abandoned vehicles and equipment everywhere on the roads, the verges and the ditches punctuated only by both military and civilian un-buried dead.

We motored on and although the threat of meeting "Gerry" and his tanks was minimal the never-ending attack by Stuka's and JU 87s with their screaming dive bombing and strafing of anything and everything was taking its toll on us, that and the clogged roads was enough for us to decide our best option of reaching Dunkirk on time was to take to the fields and open country, which we did. Making camp that night and gazing up at the blazing skyline in the far distance which was hanging over our intended destination I got a glimpse of a few stars peeping through the man-made clouds, was that the North Star? My thoughts turned to Shepherd Grace and then a jumble of memories confused my exhausted mind, Father, Mother, of course my Pamela too, will I ever get to see them again?

Next morning (25th) with Major Parkes as lead we set off,

slowly but surely we were edging toward Dunkirk, all seemed to be going well until a group of about seven or eight JU's came from nowhere and began to strafe us, the squadron scattered taking cover where best we could, the attack lasted about fifteen minutes after which Parkes appeared going like hell about a mile away, opening up and having a quick look around I discovered we were the rear tank of our now much fragmented formation which was of no real concern to me until with a screeching metallic noise from below we slewed around to the left and stopped abruptly. Shorty shouted, "Shit — think we've lost a track." Looking behind I could see his diagnoses was correct, now what? We had no joining pins and even if we had I doubt we could have repaired the track without being bumped off by something or someone and with the rest of our troop out of sight I took the decision to abandon ship and attempt to get to our destination on foot.

Relieving our metal friend of as much as we could carry, rifles, ammo and some rations we made off. We were about fifty yards away from her when there was an almighty bang, looking around I saw Sam Dempsey running away laughing, he'd dropped a grenade through the hatch to render our old friend useless to Gerry! Being in open ground in a tank is one thing, but quite another on foot so we tracked along the hedgerows, sometimes all on one side another time two of us on either, but always with one at point about fifty yards in front. Sam was at point in front of me some way when a stupid Nazi infantry man appeared from the hedge and took aim at him, before I could get my 303 to my shoulder he'd shot Sam in the back, bastard knew I was there, and as he turned to face me, I let one round off at him, that was enough and silently he fell. Almost simultaneously, two more shots rang out from the other side of the hedge which I completely ignored and ran to Sam, but he was gone. Next thing, Wilf and Eric appeared through the hedge and kneeling around Sam they told of how another Nazi ran from the hedge in front of them as I fired and they took him out. Taking a small leather pouch of valuables from his inside pocket we said farewell to our friend and made off a bit bloody quick. By my calculations I reckon we'd covered about twenty miles and with the sun beginning to set we made camp in small thicket, fortunately we still had the compo rations with us and some water.

Night fell but there was no sleep in any of us, we knew, come what may, we had to make Dunkirk tomorrow (the 26th) so when daybreak came and the sun popped its head out, we set off on what I reckoned was about a fifteen-mile journey.

As we drew closer to our destination, we arrived on some high ground and had our first glimpse of Dunkirk and the surrounding beaches, it wasn't until then we began to comprehend the enormity of what was happening. On and on we walked until we came to a junction with some Military Police (M.P.) trying to direct the overwhelming torrent of military personnel and refugees. Thinking he might know where the rest of the 7th might be we clambered over a high bank onto the road and asked the question. To our surprise and much delight, he directed us, "Keep on this road until you get to the beach, then take a left and keep going toward to port and they will be somewhere along the far end, good luck."

Just as the M.P. had finished talking a voice rang out "Wey-up, Toffee." I couldn't believe it, was it possible? The face peering over at us was Sam Denton, "What the hell are you doing here, Sam?"

"We got split from our unit a few days back when we got over-run by Germans so we've been making our way here on foot.

F*** knows what's happened to the others, that M.P told us to stay here until he calls for us to move forward." With the promise of buying him a pint in the pub when all this is over — I wished him good luck and we headed for Dunkirk, repeating the M.P.s' directions over and over in my head until thankfully we arrived at the beach. My oh my, thousands upon thousands of troops in orderly lines stretching down to the sea, wading out often up to their necks, waiting patiently to be picked up. Overhead, the Germans seemed to have a free reign of the sky again as they made run after run strafing and strafing, just carnage, but still those men stood fast and waited patiently until it was their turn to clamber aboard whatever vessel had arrived to rescue them.

We made our left turn and could see the port in the distance, everything was either on fire or in ruins and all around lay the injured and dying. We stayed focused, not stopping for anything or anyone we continued as if our conscience was non-existent. Nearing the port I heard, "Bloody hell, Wyke! We thought you lot had copped it, follow me." It was gunner Lawrence also from the 7th, we stuck behind him like leaches following his every step until we reached a ruined warehouse, "In here, lads." With little need for further encouragement, we clambered over rubble and twisted metal to a sight worth waiting for, what was left of the 7th and 4th R.T.R were here, our mates!

That night was dreadful, just continuous bombing and shelling followed by explosion after explosions and the sounds of soldiers in agony — dying, just awful. We were scheduled to leave next day (27th) on the Isle of Man Steam packet boat "Mona Isle". First light came around 0400, with no time for a brew we were on the march to Quai Felix Faure leaving everything behind save what we could carry. Once there, we joined a column of about a thousand waiting to board. We were orderly and purposeful as we made our way to the ship. It was about 0730 when we let go and were on our way to Dover, but the route out of the harbour brought us within range of several shore batteries who discharged umpteen shells at us scoring direct hits and killing many in the process.

Once out of range the next attack came by way of six Messerschmitt who repeatedly strafed us until we think they ran out of ammo and made off. By now we had taken several more direct hits and had many, many injured. HMS Windsor came alongside and their ship doctors began to treat the injured, sadly twenty-three men were killed. Dover appeared, we docked and began to disembark, and my three weeks baptism of fire was over!

At the docks we were ushered along to a Salvation Army post where a group of lovely ladies were supplying tea and cakes, the tea was drinkable but the cakes were the best ever. Listening to a Warrant Officer (W/O) with a loud hailer giving out instructions I just caught the remnants of his final call, 4th and 7th Royal Tanks follow me. Without any urgency we made an assembly and did just that finding ourselves some fifteen minutes later at the station waiting for our train. Desperate to let my family know I was back safely (I'd had no contact with them for over three weeks) I asked a waiting policeman if he could make a call home for me, at first, he was reluctant until I offered him a pound note, then obligingly he requested the telephone number and my name both of which he wrote in his note book. Eventually our train came and we clambered aboard, no rank or privilege, we were all too tired for that, we took what space we could and just collapsed in heaps of weariness.

We thought we were on our way back to Yorkshire, when word went around the carriages we were going to different camp, somewhere near Aldershot and shortly after we left the station our Major (who was going through the carriages) came across me and said, "Your French is very good, Wyke."

"Thank you, sir."

"Nearly as good as mine, where did you learn that?"

"My mother is French, sir, I have dual nationality."

"Really?"

So I asked flippantly, "Why didn't you engage the Frenchman then sir?"

"I was enjoying watching you handle him," he mischievously replied, we both had a chuckle at that. Then he said how he thought we'd copped it and I spoke of how we lost a track etc, then lost Sam as we made our way on foot to the port, surprisingly he asked, "Where did you go, Wyke?"

"Roysses, sir — in Abingdon."

"Ha, I was just down the road at Radley, well that was a bloody good show Wyke, excellent stuff."

"Thank you, sir, is it correct that we're not going back to Catterick, sir?"

"Tweseldown Wyke." And walked away.

Tweseldown it was then? Arriving at our new camp we were allocated our billets and simply conked out utterly exhausted, lord knows how long most of us slept for but I can tell you I didn't hear Reveille! We had four days of winding down in which much discussion took place among all ranks as to the performance of our equipment, tanks, ammo, rations, clothing, W/T's etc all came up for scrutiny after which we were given seven day's leave! First stop, the Post Office in Hendred to see my Pamela who was as beautiful and graceful as ever. It was a joyous re-union for sure, then on to Windy Ridge and home. Mother was in tears and Father, a man of few words. shook my hand and gave me a hug. Pamela joined us for our evening meal after which father suggested we went to the Eyston Arms in the village to celebrate my return. We're not a family of drinkers, in fact I don't ever recall Father going to a pub so that was an occasion in itself, even more-so when Pamela's parents joined us. All was going well until old man Denton walked in, he came over to us and not in his usual intimidating manner announced, "My Sam is dead — killed." We were all speaking to him of our sadness when he took from his pocket the telegram — *It is with much regret I have to inform you on the 21st of May near Arras your son Samuel Isaac Denton was reported missing presumed killed, it was signed by the C.O of Royal Berkshire Regiment —*

"That's wrong, that's wrong," I said, "I bumped into Sam just outside Dunkirk on the 26th!"

"What? Are you kidding me?" Old man Denton said.

"Not at all, on the 21st we were in Arass and I recall seeing on our battle plan map the R.Bs were to the north of us in the thick of things and I remember thinking of Sam then because I knew they were being ripped to pieces, I was so surprised to see him five days later near Dunkirk, he was with five or six of his mates who'd got there on foot after losing their unit, we had a conversation and even joked about buying each other a pint here one day."

"So where is my son now then?"

"Well, for certain he wasn't killed on the 21st, clearly, he didn't make it across so my best guess is if he wasn't killed at Dunkirk, he's been taken a Prisoner of War (POW.)?"

Mr Denton's eyes filled with tears, "My God, I pray so — I pray so, thank you, you've given my family hope," then he left. As my seven day leave drew to an end and considering all my kit was already there and the weather forecast was okay, I decided to go back to camp on my 350 AJS. Arriving at the camp entrance an M.P. stopped me: "Name?"

"L/Cpl Wyke."

"Ah, just one moment while I check — yes and you are to report to your Warrant Officer (W/O) immediately." Thinking, 'Oh dear, what can I have done wrong?' I made to his office and nervously knocked. "Come — Ah, Wyke, don't unpack I have a note here from the C.O stating you are to report to the Selection Board tomorrow at 0900."

"Oh why?"

"Probably because someone has nominated you for a commission."

"Bloody hell."

"That's what I thought, Wyke — you are to present yourself to the selection board tomorrow morning for three days of interrogation — off you go back home and good luck." Three hours after leaving home I was back! Next day I drove myself in Mother's car to a sprawling country house in Sussex for my "interrogation" and I could see how that initial meeting could have been quite intimidating for some, four officers and a man in a suit (who I later found out was a psychiatrist) randomly quizzing me reminded me of Roysses, but I felt confident about myself.

My first task for the afternoon was to write a self-description in one hour. Easy enough I thought, just be truthful. Next day and next task, was an intelligence test — maths, puzzle solving and the like followed by an observation test, then a quick reaction test and that was day two over. The final test on the morning of day three was pretty intense, they called it performance under stress and it was just that, locked in a darkened "cupboard", headphones and microphone with instructions and events being screamed at you together with a background noise of battle, after that was a mock interrogation, all pretty realistic. Then lunch and back to the panel for another interview and review of my performance followed by a thank you very much you will receive the panel's decision within seven days. Home again!

Chapter Five

Sandhurst to S.O.E.

Six days later and a brown enveloped letter arrived, saying I'd been accepted for a commission to the Royal Military Academy, Sandhurst! So thrilled with that news, Father went out next day and bought me my first car, a 1936 MG TA in green which conveyed me safely there and after a lightning tour of the place I made to my room but was a tad disappointed to find it was a double sharing room, fortunately my new roommate was a good type and we got on very well.

Later in the day our Captain gave our group a rundown of what we were to expect which was basically four courses, three of four-week duration and the fourth a six-week course. The first course was similar to my training with the Royal Berkshires, all about infantry and in the field stuff which included a trip to Brecon Beacons and a couple of nights under canvas, all pretty straightforward. Then there was a Gunnery course with a trip down to Purbright and again most of which I'd covered during my time with the 7th. Next, radio training which I really enjoyed, not least because this was another subject I'd covered with the 7th. The final six weeks was a culmination of the previous courses, over and over again, surprisingly though only a short time was spent studying subjects like rules of engagement and interpretation of orders etc, but a rule that did disappoint me was once commissioned you were not allowed to return to your previous regiments!

Mid November 1940 was my passing-out parade, a pretty low-key event with no family present, apparently, I'd made good grades and surprisingly ended up as a Second Lieutenant. Directly after the Parade I was summoned to see the captain.

It was a strange conversation to say the least:

"Wyke — another unit of His Majesties Services have requested they interview you."

"Really, sir? What for, sir?"

"Haven't a clue other than you are to report to 27 Beaumont Street, Oxford at 1000 hours tomorrow. Oh, and in civilian clothes too — once there you are to ask for an appointment to see the dentist."

"But my teeth are fine, sir."

"All will be revealed Wyke and not a word to any one — close the door behind you."

"Yes sir."

Next day in the heart of the university town I found number 27, a fine house among similar Regency buildings. Pressing the inter-com button, a well-spoken female voice asked, "May I help you?"

"I would like to make an appointment to see the dentist please?" Next thing, the door opened and I was gestured in, "Follow me please, Mr Wilmslow will see you now." Such mystery.

"Ah, Mr Wyke." enquired a smartly dressed ginger-haired gentleman, sat behind a huge leather-topped desk.

"I am indeed he."

"Good, you will be familiar with the Official Secrets Act, won't you?"

"Very much so."

"Good, a unit has been created on the orders of the P.M, its purpose, by means of espionage, sabotage and reconnaissance is quite simply to cause as much chaos and damage as possible to the enemy machine throughout Axis occupied Europe and beyond and also to make contact with resistance organisations to train and equip them. Naturally, these special tasks take special people and it has been suggested you might just be the type of person we want. Apparently, you're fluent in French and have dual nationality with connections in the Loire and you've tasted conflict too? But it is purely voluntary, no one will order you to partake, indeed you are free to leave as and when you wish. But be under no illusion these would be dangerous times, mostly you would be operating on your own and in an occupied country.

"You have forty-eight hours to think about it, if you want to join then telephone me, if I do not hear from you within that time, I will assume you have declined — not a word, Mr Wyke, not a word, cheerio then".

By the time I'd got back to Windy Ridge I'd pretty much made my mind up to join whatever it was Wilmslow was suggesting. The excitement and sense of adventure was overwhelming any of the dangers he spoke of, but what on earth was I to tell Pamela and my parents? All three of them knew of my interview, but not its purpose so my bluff was to say I've been offered a job, training new recruits, but it would entail being away from home for considerable amounts of time and although the being away part wasn't that well received the thought of me not being in conflict certainly pleased them. I made that call and the very obliging Wilmslow asked me back to his office ASAP!

Back in Wilmslow's Oxford office I found he was a little more enlightening, almost revealing in fact.

"You are now a candidate for the Special Operations Executive and your six-month training programme will begin immediately — do you still have your rail warrant?"

"I do."

"Good, you need to get to Fort William in the Highlands,

once there, transport will take you to Arisaig House where you will be part of training Group A, plan to be there for four weeks at least — good luck."

Two days later I'm at a bitterly cold Fort William station and as promised was met, then driven some distance to Arisaig House, a stunning cross between a castle and a medieval house set in acres of spectacular scenery, but before anything I was taken to an interview room and told the rules.

Remove all rank and regimental insignia from uniforms, under no circumstances exchange or disclose any personal information — to anyone. No contact with the outside world for the duration of your stay, no photography and so it went on after which I was shown my billet where there were two other guys already installed and a third yet to arrive (four to a hut). Eventually he did and although we all got on well and chatted profusely, we consciously stuck to the rules. There were several other huts dotted about the place with mostly groups of four in each, and although we were not allowed to converse with any other huts, we knew by their accent some were Norwegian?

The next four weeks were all about tortuous Commando training, which I have to say at times I felt like giving up on! Umpteen mountain treks with full pack while endeavouring to keep up with the Commando leading us. Scaling sheer cliff faces, gruelling assault courses, simulated being tracked down on the run across bleak terrain etc pushing us to the very limit of physical endurance. Armed combat instruction included the use of our Fairbairn knives, hand and sten guns, grenades etc as well as un-armed combat which was all about every unsavoury but silent way one could think of to dispatch someone!

From Scotland to Manchester and No. 1 Parachute Training School (P.T.S.) where I had a week to learn how to parachute! The course culminated in a static line jump from a Balloon and another at two thousand feet from a Dakota.

By now it was spring 1941 and with a crash course of Commando Para-Military training behind me as well as two jumps I was on my way to the other end of the country for my Group B training in the splendour of Beaulieu House, in the New Forrest.

Just as in Scotland there were numerous huts scattered around the estate each specializing in their own unique subjects.

My first being communications where fortunately my time with the 7th, Sandhurst and OTC Roysses had already taught me much about the subject including Morse Code, but not how to repair the various types of wireless in use. The recognisance hut was interesting — how to sketch a map and knowing what features to include. Decoy and observation — how to check if you were being followed and how to lose them (we would practise this in near-by Bournemouth). But by far the most intriguing was sabotage and demolition, which apart from learning how to use plastic explosives (P.E.) with very short fuses was much about selecting a target which caused the most disruption (blow up a telegraph pole that could be replaced in a few hours or a transformer that could knock a town out for a few weeks). There was even a one-day course on how to pick locks given, we were told, by a formidable "ex" Con.

Then there was tuition on how to live a clandestine life, to melt into the surroundings, to be inconspicuous, (rarely do you see a Frenchman with his hands in his pockets) and of course what to and what not to do under interrogation, just so much to take in.

July 1941 and apparently, I had attained the acquired levels of skills so my time at camp B had come to an end and a small but adequate flat had been arranged for me near Boscombe where I was to reside until such time as I will be called upon, but I could come and go as I please — needless to say my direction was home.

At speed in my little green rocket, it didn't take long before I arrived back at Windy Ridge and what a welcome that was, I'd telephoned home the day before so it was of no surprise to see Pamela and Mother waiting at the door. Lots of hugs and kisses and where have you been-s? Later, Father appeared, we sat and chatted for ages, so much to catch up on, "How is the Shepherd?"

"Fine." Then some welcome news the Red Cross had contacted the Denton's to say Sam was indeed a POW.

It was the end of August and to make the most of the remnants of summer I took Pamela out for a drive and picnic in the countryside, it was one of those days one never wanted to end which reminded me of the Shepherds favourite saying, "Nothing lasts forever", sadly it didn't and all to soon I was saying my cheerio's.

Big hug and tears from Mother and a gentlemanly hand shake from Father along with, "Take good care of yourself, Son." Together with a 'you don't fool me' look!

Dropping Pamela off at her home en-route our good-bye was as much painful as tearful, all the time I was trying to make light of our parting but I got the distinct impression from Pamela her thoughts were this could be our last good-bye!

The drive back to Boscombe was a blur of thoughts and emotions, not least in my mind was Wilmslow's promise I could withdraw at any moment, but my stupid sense of adventure overpowered any such thoughts.

Chapter Six

First Operation

Each night in my flat I could hear the Luftwaffe constantly bombing the south coast ports of Portsmouth, Southampton, Poole and Weymouth and I could clearly see the orange skies and the stair rod like lines of the search lights together with the thunderous noise which even this far away was horrendous, pity the poor souls living there. But that nightly distraction was ended by a call from non-other than Wilmslow. "A car will pick you up tomorrow at 0900, time to put all that training into practise and the very best of luck to you." 0900 and I'm on my way — somewhere?

"Where are we going, driver?"

"Bedfordshire, sir, that's all I can tell you."

Eventually arriving at what was clearly an RAF base we drew up at a very run-down building, more like a farm house than a camp HQ. Nevertheless, it was considerably better inside than out.

Thus began my briefing, two men in suits and a Captain who politely introduced themselves by code name only, once done they gave me my code name — Ferret, simple. Then the captain laid a huge map of France out. "Tomorrow night you will be dropped into occupied France, the exact location is not yet known but we will cover that tomorrow afternoon in your final briefing.

"The RAF are losing pilots and air crew quicker than they

can be replaced and not necessarily because they are being killed in action, quite the contrary, the attrition is because they are unable to get back here after they've come down, so the creation of reliable and effective escape routes for them is vital and that's where you come in Ferret.

"At present there is an established route, the "Comete Line" from Holland through Belgium to Paris and then southward via Orleans- Bordeaux and on to the Pyrenees and into Spain, but we need another route to cover the Normandy and Brittany coasts then heading south toward Nantes/Laval — Bordeaux where it can pick up with Comete and on to Sans Sebastian or Pau and ideally running parallel to the coast? Your drop will be blind, that's to say no one will be on the ground to welcome you because we are yet to establish reliable contact with any resistance organisations in that region.

"Your cover story is your family farm was destroyed and your parents killed in the fighting near Arras in May 1940 and you will have papers to confirm that. Since then, you have been making your way as far from the conflict as possible, you will be looking for work on farms while establishing contacts with the local resistance and sympathisers. Paramount is the creation off another escape route, secondary is to create chaos for the enemy however you so desire.

"Can you confirm you have already been given your cover name, papers and I.D documents appertaining to that?"

"Yes, I have."

"Good, well that's enough for today, get a good night's sleep and we will resume here tomorrow at 1000 hours."

Next morning, with everything connecting the old me to the new me, including my clothes safely stored, I donned my French-made clothing and shoes. So, I began my new life as Eric Garnier and as such my first stop was to collect my kit consisting of my Colt 32, 1 L tablet (Cyanide) 4 Benzedrine tabs that extended my awake time. Fairbairn knife, money belt, steno-code sheet, contact list, map and code grid, first aid kit, binoculars, some wire, tape, pliers and a pair of dark brown overalls to make the drop in, oh and small fold up shovel to bury my chute with.

The final briefing was pretty intense, going over and over my I.D. and cover story along with the escape line route I was to adhere to as best I could. Lunch came and went and yet more briefing began but by now my brain was in overload, although I knew pretty much what was expected of me. It was about 1600 hours and the suggestion was I should get some sleep for a few hours, which believe it or not I did.

1900 hours and a sharp knock on my door reminded me of why I was here! Gathering my thoughts while pulling on my overalls and looking at the heap of kit I was to somehow squeeze into a webbing belt that supposedly had enough pockets for the job. I eventually made my way back to the briefing room where my three "instructors" were waiting and we exchanged in some small talk while waiting for my wireless set to arrive. By now it was around 2100 hours and a welcome bowl of soup with ample bread appeared and even though I was beginning to feel extremely sick I soon consumed the lot.

Right — ready? I was so nervous that my mouth wouldn't work, so I nodded approvingly. The cool September night air struck me as we walked to the aircraft, a Whitley bomber. Next, a P.T. instructor lifted my chute onto my back and secured it fast, "A toddy aforyougo," said the captain, and they all watched me down whatever it was in one, "Good luck, old boy," someone said as I boarded. Hatch shut, engines revved and we were taxing out, then flat out and up, no turning back now!

The navigator said, "We are making for an area south of Vire, Normandy, our route was far from direct, instead we headed across country to Weymouth then across the channel to the left of the Channel Islands making land near St Malo, the flight time is about one and a half hours, the drop will be at 1500 feet, so about a forty second ride for you!" What seemed like an age later the navigator instructed back, "Five minutes to drop off!" Checking and double checking I had everything especially my wireless set I positioned myself next to the drop hatch, "Hatch open!" and my feet were dangling into the night sky while the static line was being attached, "60 seconds — 30 — 20 — Go!" and I was out of the aircraft not knowing if I jumped or was pushed. First thoughts — 'Chute open? Yes, flippin cold!'

With the Whitley already out of sight and sound, I hit the ground and rolled to my side in the process, checking legs, feet, toes, arms and hands were still attached and working I looked to pull my set in which was attached to me via a longish rope. Everything intact and realising I was in the middle of a very big ploughed field, I made for the nearest cover where I buried my chute in a hedgerow.

By my reckoning, it was after midnight but not knowing exactly where I was, I decided to curl into the hedgerow and wait till day break before moving on. With not an ounce of sleep in me and scared witless I drew comfort at finding the North Star and thinking of home.

Stirring around daybreak to a mild frost and thinking what a good idea it was to have kept my overalls on I crawled quietly out of the hedgerow and once standing I could for the first time see the terrain about me. Scanning with my binoculars I discovered I'd come down in the middle of a huge freshly ploughed field, in the distance, a hill with small woods a top, while in the opposite direction a valley which was very overgrown in places and immediately the other side of the hedge was a what looked like a little used farm track — my route away?

Overalls off and clutching dearly my wireless case, I set off going downhill — why that way I'll never know.

Glancing down the valley I could see a man walking in my direction with what looked like a couple of rabbits?

At that point I don't think he'd seen me but not knowing for sure I decided to carry on walking and see how things develop. There was a gate in the distance, and I figured at this rate we would run into each other about there, which indeed we did. "Bonjour," he said, and I replied the same but added, "Rabbit for breakfast?"

"No this is for dinner, eggs are for breakfast, what are you doing here so early, have you been sleeping rough?"

"Yes, I have, I'm making my way south but it got dark very quickly so I decided to sleep here."

"Come join me for breakfast — you must be ready for that." And together we walked off down the track, he was a Mediterranean looking man, stocky, in his late thirties perhaps and a bit grubby but instantly there was something about him I liked, I asked him if he was local and what he did. Apparently, he was a blacksmith come mechanic with a forge/workshop attached to his house which we were just about to arrive at.

It was an old stone cottage, very small and situated behind his garage and small forecourt right on a T junction. Going inside it was like stepping back in time, a huge wood burning range dominated the kitchen area, no sink, just an outside water pump. In the corner was a very questionable staircase leading to lord knows what. While he (Rafael) disappeared for some eggs I decided to skin the rabbits and had almost finished the pair by the time he came in, much to his amusement and approval.

He boiled six eggs and delivered me three along with a chunk of bread he tore from a stick, rough it was, but tasty and very welcome.

He asked about my past, where I came from etc and I told him I was from Arras but had lost everything including my family in the fighting the previous year, there was something a bit mysterious about him and every time I probed him for similar information, he either ignored me or changed the subject. After breakfast he showed me his workshop and explained how he was going to repair the old Renault tractor there that had broken its half shaft. I felt really comfortable with Rafael, I think he enjoyed having some company and we were getting on very well when surprisingly he asked if I would like to stay a few days and went on to say I could have the room upstairs as he usually slept on the sofa after "One or two" glasses of his home-made Calvados.

Willingly accepting his invitation, I was relieved I had found what seemed like a safe base for a few days. Rafael suggested I spend the day exploring as he had to finish the tractor, agreeing with his suggestion I asked if I could have a look upstairs and make myself comfortable there (my intention being to send my first message back). "Of course. I'll see you around lunch time then," he said.

Back in the cottage and upstairs into what I though was once a hay loft, there were no windows but a sack door at one end and a bed of sorts at the other, but it was more than adequate. Opening up my wireless case, gleefully seeing all was still intact, I prepared to send my first wireless transmission, with much excitement I tapped in my recognition code — no response. Then again — nothing. I re-checked the frequency settings and sent again — nothing. Now what? I didn't want to leave the set on for fear of being detected so I turned off and waited for ten minutes before trying again. Switch on, frequency check, send message — wait — then a flurry of Morse back confirming my message had been received followed by the switch off code which was then followed by a big sigh of relief from me, I was now up and running!

It was around four p.m. when Rafael came into the kitchen, he'd finished the tractor and been paid too so out came the Calvados, but before I'd taken a sip I asked about dinner, "What are we having and who's cooking?"

Pointing to the rabbits he said, "You skinned them, my friend, so you cook them!"

"Okay," I said, searching for a roasting tray and some fat but only finding two saucepans I concluded we were having boiled rabbit with onions and potato, which a couple of hours later we did!

By now Rafael was "warm" with drink and beginning to talk more freely which I of course I encouraged him to do as I had already detected a difficult past and a hatred of all things German.

Eventually I decided to come straight out and ask him. "So, tell me about your journey, Rafael. What brought you, a Spaniard, here and why are you so insular?"

"Okay, my friend, I trust you, I was Pascal Laurent from Corsica, you know where that is?"

"Yes, an island south of Marseilles — north of Sardinia."

"Correct, my friend, I was living at home and working as a mechanic, I had a beautiful girlfriend, my fiancé, we were to be married but I found she was cheating on me, my friends all knew but didn't tell me. I felt humiliated and decided to leave the island, at that time there was talk of civil war in Spain so fearing nothing to lose and seeking adventure I took the ferry to the mainland then a train to Toulouse, from there to Pau then made my way to Bilbao where I joined with the separatist foreign fighters.

"Franco hated us, labelling us mercenaries, although we had many battles with his republican army, we mostly did sabotage work. We were near the town of Guernica when Franco's fascist friend Adolf Hitler sent in the bombers, they deliberately picked market day knowing the town would have many civilian visitors from the villages. We arrived shortly after the bombings, the town was full of dead and dying people, many of them women and children, it was awful my friend, awful. On the way back to Bilbao I was taken prisoner and put in a cell in a small police station with another separatist. He was Basque and pretty fearless, he said we were to be shot next day and had to get out somehow? Next thing he fell to the floor and began writhing about in agony, holding his stomach, the guard came (there was only one on duty) I gestured to him for help, stupidly he came in and stooped over my cell mate and realising this was my only opportunity to escape I grabbed him around the neck and squeezed as hard as I could for what seemed ages and as I did so my cell mate sprung to life and covered the guards mouth, eventually the guard became unconscious but still I held tight until he died.

"Our escape was successful and we made our way back to Bilbao, fortunately there were many sympathisers on the way who gave us food and shelter and I stayed in the area until the civil war was all but over. Not wanting to go back to Corsica or stay in Spain to face a possible murder charge I decided to go to the northwest of France. I wrote a letter to my mother making out it was from a friend of mine explaining how Pascal had been killed fighting with the separatists in Spain, I destroyed my French passport and that is my journey my friend and why I hate the Germans. So now I am free and all those who once knew me believe I'm dead!" Nodding with amazement, he said, "Remember, my friend, nothing lasts forever."

I asked Rafael how he got here and why the Spanish name?

"My friends in Bilbao created me a new Spanish I.D card and passport in the name of Rafael Garcia, from Madrid, not from Basque country so Franco's murderers would leave me alone and if I settled in France my Spanish passport would keep me out of the French army."

"Did The Basques have a path across the Pyrenees?"

"Yes, it was used for bringing in arms from France."

"Is that how you crossed?"

"Yes, their guide led me and three other Frenchmen me across."

"So how did you come to be here, at this place?"

"When I was with the Basques, we didn't just wage war, to do that we needed arms to get them we needed money, to get that we robbed banks, then getting up from the table he pulled the bottom drawer out of the cooker, put his hand inside and withdrew a floor board, he put his hand back in again and pulled out a leather bag, here catch — I did and opened it — it was full of bank notes, some Spanish but mostly French. You think I was stupid enough not to keep a little back?" We both laughed and celebrated his journey with another glass.

"But how did you buy this place?"

"Like you I was making this way, sleeping rough when I came across it, it was boarded up but a couple were looking around it, not expecting an answer I jokingly said is it for sale? 'It could be,' they answered and went on to say they were from near Paris and had been left it in a will by an uncle they never knew, "So how much then?" 'Five thousand Francs,' they replied. No, much too expensive, we are in a war, I give you one thousand in cash — When? Now if you want! They showed me around and asked how would I pay so I opened that bag and counted out one thousand Francs, there you are but I need the deeds — we have them here, and I will need a bill of sale, a receipt and a letter transferring the deeds, we can do that now they said and that my friend is how I got this place, I am on no register anywhere, I am invisible and that's how I like to be."

"What happened to the other three with you?"

"One went to live near Pau and the other two stayed in Bordeaux when we stopped there on our journey north."

"Are you still in touch with them?"

"Only the two in Bordeaux."

All of that said, we carried on drinking like old friends until we'd both had more than enough, I went to my bed and Rafael his sofa. Next morning having absorbed most of what Rafael had divulged I decided I had enough information on him to disclose part of my reason for being here. "Rafael — there is something about me you need to know, who I am and the real reason I'm here."

"Let me guess," he said with a smile, "You are a British Spy."

"What?"

He went on to say, "I heard your plane low and guessed it was a parachute drop, that's why I was out early in the morning and when you went out yesterday afternoon, I searched the loft and I found your wireless set!"

Chapter Seven

A Very Good Friend

Having listened to Raphael's story, some of which I found spurious to say the least, I'd decided to be quite guarded as to why I was in France, at least for the time being. He knew I was British and working behind the lines and he knew of my wireless too but not much else so I said my purpose was to gather information on troop movements, in particular tank and armour and if possible, to make contact with resistance groups.

"So you want to make contact with the resistance my friend? I can help you with that. We have a small group who cover this area, we have contact with a group in Nantes and my friends in Bordeaux are very active there to. But how can you, the British, help us?"

My answer was basically once I was confident these were genuine people I could arrange for an arms and ammunition drop and could even arrange a small amount of money, his response was to offer to take me to Nantes tomorrow, but looking at the map I suggested it too far for one day, "Why not meet in Rennes which is about half way?" He was okay with that but it would take some time to organise, perhaps two days' time? With his approval I messaged back to base — much progress — contact with R (resistance) in 4 ref C 6 (which was that area grid code) out.

Three days later and I was on the bus to Rennes, I was to meet a man and a woman from the resistance on the Pont de Rennes Bridge. Fortunately, I had been to the centre before with Mother and Auntie so I had a rough idea of where things were. It was fairly busy there but it didn't take long for me to find them standing over the centre arch as agreed. Without Raphael as a go between the conversation was understandably slow and very guarded but eventually as we walked and talked some mutual trust began to emerge.

We talked for about thirty minutes on how we could benefit each other and I explained how we needed accurate information on Nazi movements at the port of St Nazaire. They suggested they could supply that info but went on to say they were in desperate need of arms and ammunition, so with the promise of delivering such to them and training on the use of new plastic explosives we went our separate ways. In all it was a good meeting.

That night back at Raphael's I sent a W/T to base telling how I had met the resistance group from Nantes and concluded they were genuine, relaying also of how they offer a reliable source of info on Nazi activity at the port of St Nazaire, but that they needed arms etc and a wireless set. My message was well received by B.S. and they went on to say they would organise a supply drop but would not provide a wireless at this point in time!

The next few days passed trouble-free and as pre-planned I contacted base only to be given the excellent news a supply drop was to be made in seven days' time at 1100 hours with a code grid reference that pinpointed a field just east of the village of Couffè (which was north of Nantes). Raphael wanted to relay the message personally and set off first thing next day to do so. With my all be-it new contacts made in the Nantes area my attention turned to Bordeaux and the equally important question of how am I to get these fairly autonomous groups to come together as one? Trust was the by word especially because of the very real threat of being infiltrated, not just by the Gestapo but by collaborators of the Vichy too.

Part of the plan was to implement a structure where-by members can only communicate within a group with two other people, from group to group it was only by a nominated member of each group to the opposite nominated member of another, adhering to these simple rules would minimise infiltration and exposure.

Two days after the drop to the Nantes group Raphael made the journey to see for himself the outcome, later that day he returned home bursting with excitement not only because of the riffles and bren guns that had been dropped, but because the stranger he had introduced into their circle had proved good, however they were not entirely pleased with the fact there were no explosives nor wireless, which led me to quickly explain the UK had a temporary supply problem but assuring him they would be included in the next drop.

Thinking about the situation at hand, Raphael and his group had pretty much Normandy, including the Cherbourg Peninsular, and Brittany covered. The Nantes group reached northward toward Raphael and southwards reaching the yet to be established Bordeaux group, the only fly in the ointment being I was based too far north near Vire and Raphael appreciated that so it was decided I should temporarily move south around Cholet, which would place me pretty much in the centre of my area.

But before my relocation I sent a message to base with a plea for explosives and a radio set for the Nantes group without which they couldn't function. To my amazement, this was agreed and another drop was successfully made. Two days after the drop I was in their camp in the Loire Valley doing a quick course on wireless operation along with explaining their codes and Morse book etc and an even quicker course on plastic explosives!

Bordeaux was concerning me, it was a long way south and bordering the Vichy zone where people had been spared much of the fighting so far and its puppet ruler, fascist sympathiser Marshal Petain had been given autonomy to govern.

On capitulation some of the French army there had changed sides as did much of their Mediterranean Fleet. It was a place where no one could be trusted but I felt I had to make the journey to see first-hand who we were potentially dealing with.

Raphael provided my route; it was a two-day journey by local buses with a night stop in a moderate guest house at Niort. Arriving late morning next day, I made my way to the port area looking for the Tabac Le Pacha. Once found and seated the waiter nodded for my attention. "Cafe for my friend Raphael please," was the word, at which point he made about to the rear of the shop through a swing door which immediately swung back the other way by the force of two men coming from the opposite direction!

"Cafe Raphael for you."

"Please," they gestured with slight sideways nod of the head to follow them. Before going to the Tabac I spent a good half an hour on the opposite bank surveying the general area, gladly it appeared safe so I followed them out of the building and along the wharf to a pot shed, a knock on the door, it opened and we three went inside. The conversation that followed was much the same as with the Nantes group, they needed arms and equipment of which I said I could supply and train them to, I then went on to say how I'd made contact with Nantes and it is vital that the three groups (including Raphael) should liaise with each other to bring about maximum effect and they agreed saying they would send one of their group to a map location roughly half way to Nantes in seven days' time at mid-day to establish a line of communication, excellent!

Meeting over and they walked with me back to the bus station and I remarked about there being no Germans anywhere and also asked about a group of people in a queue over there, pointing to a rather forlorn looking assembly of about forty, mostly women and children. They were Jews being sent to Germany, it was part of Petain's obligation to Hitler!

Thankfully my bus journey back to Raphael's was as uneventful as the one down to Bordeaux, including my night stop.

Raphael was brimming with questions about his comrades in Bordeaux and the outcome of my meeting. With much excitement we chatted for hours about what appeared to be the newly formed coherent force that theoretically exists from Normandy all the way to the Spanish border! Later that night I sent news of my work back to base along with a request for the equipment drop I promised our new friends in Bordeaux which was confirmed with an undertaking it would be made sometime within the next two weeks, in fact during my contact with base next day they provided the date, time and grid reference for the Bordeaux drop which fortunately was three days after the pre-arranged meeting with the Nantes group, so I decided to meet with the later and give them the news to relay to their new friends from the south thereby reinforcing the good will and trust between all groups.

Thinking too about names for each group, Vire was now Pole, Nantes was Orion and Bordeaux was Vega and our escape line was to be Star.

By now it was Christmas 1941 and things were looking good, my three groups were established and communicating with each other, the Vega group had successfully blown up an MT boat in the Port and Orion had identified a rail bridge they wanted to blow! Now at last my attention can focus on what was supposed to have been my priority for being there and that was to create an escape route south.

So far, the most successful line was the Comete Line to Bordeaux and then on to Spain and my initial instructions was for our new line from the north to link up with the Comete Line at Bordeaux, then onto Spain. However, I was very aware the Comete line was predominantly a non-confrontational organisation, not pacifists but sympathisers to the Allied cause and as such they would not take up arms. The problem now being my three groups were very much resistance fighters and the slightest hint of sharing anything with any one not prepared to die for the cause was out of the question, the only solution (as they suggested) was "their own" line, one that was entirely organised and run by them.

Understanding their position completely and being reminded too that they had several fishing boats at their disposal from La-Rochelle all the way to Spain, all of which were capable of transporting "Passengers" to Bilbao led me to believe this idea was good, but Baker Street (B.S) might need some convincing.

Next W/T, I put the idea of our new line and the reasons behind it to B.S who said they needed time to study and consider my proposal (and names) before they would confirm, understandable I suppose.

At breakfast a couple of days later we heard a car draw up followed by several bangs on the door.

"It's okay," Raphael said reassuringly, "I know him," and he let the extremely excited man in.

"Raphael, I have two airmen — they came down near me last night and knocked my door — what shall I do?"

"Okay," Raphael said while grabbing his coat, "I will follow you back and take care of the situation," and as he was going through the door, he turned to me and said, "Looks like we have our first customers!"

Not being able to contain myself, I sent the following W/T to base, two aircrew at Pole — details to follow — star line operational, almost immediately the reply was — 'Congrats Ferret'.

It was mid-afternoon before Raphael returned with so much to say, the two were Canadians, their Halifax was returning from a raid on St Nazaire when they got hit the pilot ordered abandon which they did, but they noted they were the only ones to bail out, as they did, they could see their aircraft, although on fire, continuing to fly until they lost sight of it. He had the aircraft serial number and their service numbers and went on to say he had installed them in a safe house where they can be collected by Orion tomorrow. Excellent work!

Base was informed of the service numbers of the fliers and serial number of the Halifax and Orion given details of the rendezvous.

January was relatively quiet mostly because the very bad weather had put a stop to flights and the frozen ground would leave clear trails of where my "Maquis" friends had been, but excellent news from base was to confirm the first success of Star Line — the two Canadians had made it to the Spanish border and on to Gibraltar, then safely back to GB.

February and things began to get going again, Vega successfully sabotaged a fuel supply line to the port and Pole "collected" three airmen and installed them on Star Line. Although Orion were quiet on the fighting front their information gathering on the Port of St Nazaire was vitally important. Toward the end of the month and quite out of the blue base said my work here was considered done and they would be making plans to recover me, but that should remain most secret.

March came and I began to get a flurry of messages from base, but interestingly Orion (Nantes) were instructed not undertake any sabotage or similar activity until further notice which led me to believe something big was in the offing and they didn't want to draw any unnecessary attention to that area. A few days later came the news I didn't want to hear, which was to rendezvous with a Lysander recovery plane on the 24th!

It was the 20th and just four days prior to my planned departure when myself and Orion received some very specific instructions, at precisely 1145 hours on the night of the 27th they were to knock out a search light and AA gun emplacement on the Loire estuary at Saint Marc, reason — at 0005, just twenty minutes later, there was to be a substantial air raid on the port of St Nazaire.

The following day we both received instructions they were, if possible, to plant delayed explosives on the two bridges in the town that cross the river Le Brevit, the delay should be set for 0900 hours on the 28th, so why was I being recalled was my question to base. Because it was an order, was the reply.

So, it was at 2300 hours on the night of the 24th. I stood in a field with my very good friend Raphael waiting for my taxi back to blighty. Almost silently the little fly like aircraft fell from the sky and landed, a quick hug from Raphael, the side door opened and before I was even fully inside, we were turning about and speeding over the grass, up this little fly climbed and homeward bound was I.

It was a crisp early morning when we landed back at Bedfordshire, and although I slept for most of the journey, I felt exhausted and the chaps there could see that so they took me to a room with a bed where I collapsed until around 1000 hours when I was woken by an orderly with tea and toast. That willingly consumed I made for the de-briefing room for a short interview ending with a well done, we will be in touch shortly. Thankfully someone had put my car in one of the hangers and with a couple of long pushes it burst into life, and I was on my way home!

Chapter Eight

First Face to Face!

My drive back home was full of thoughts and reminisces of my time in France, I'd made a successful drop into the French night sky which led to my chance meeting with Raphael and all that encounter brought about: Three separate resistance groups were now operating as one joined up force, the Star line was operational and I had a good feeling about my work there during which time, fortune or not I hadn't had one face to face encounter with Gerry. My MG was positively purring by the time I made the turn of the main road into Hendred, but what will Pamela and my parents think of me for not communicating with them for so long? As I turned up the slight rise to the Post Office, Pamela came running out of the shop, arms aloft and screaming with excitement — holding back the tears — "Seb, Seb, where have you been?" etc and after an extremely long and emotional hugging (which I'm sure half the village witnessed) she released her hold on me saying over and over, "We must go to Windy Ridge now," and so we did. With hand on horn as I drew up, Mother came to the door and just exploded with pent up emotion, tears followed sobs followed by more and more tears, it was very moving, as we moved inside, she shouted across to one of the hands to fetch Father, "Sebastian is back!"

It was a moving moment when father arrived, he just shook my hand warmly and said, "Welcome back, son, we missed you."

And I think I detected a tear roll down his cheek.

Euphoria was followed by the inevitable "Where have you been all these months and why didn't you write?"

"Oh, I've been in Canada in the middle of nowhere training new recruits."

"But surely you could have contacted us somehow?" Mother asked, "Father said he would have Monique if he could, now let's leave that subject and enjoy now."

It was teatime two days later when news came over the wireless of a spectacular raid on the dock yard at St Nazaire. Immediately I was all ears and demanded silence. Apparently, an old Royal Navy ship disguised as a Nazi one with several hundred Commandos on board sailed up the Loire estuary to the dockyard and rammed the gates of the huge dry dock, once straddling the dock gates the Commandos leapt ashore and caused havoc to the dock infrastructure, hand to hand fighting continued for many hours before most of the Commandos made their escape to several R.N ships waiting at sea. But with precise timing minutes before the operation (Code named Chariot) took place a team of resistance fighters, known as the Maquis successfully destroyed search lights and gun emplacements situated at the mouth of the estuary, next, at exactly the pre-arranged time several squadrons of Halifax's from Bomber Command bombed strategic targets around the Port, the bulletin went on to say the Maquis also blew up two bridges over the river Le-Brivet preventing reinforcements reaching the dockyard. The operation, which had taken months of meticulous planning and with cooperation of many units of the French resistance, was a complete success. "Excellent stuff," I said with much excitement.

"Nothing to do with you, son?" Father said, looking me in the eye.

"Hardly — I've been in Canada, Father, remember?" Then came a look only a father could give a son.

With the two weeks leave Baker Street had given me drawing to a close it was time to bid Pamela and my parents goodbye again, leaving home and Pamela with spring unfolding was not easy, but with a promise to keep them all informed as to my whereabouts, a promise I knew I couldn't keep.

We exchanged farewells, kisses and hugs and off I drove, it was then the reality of it all hit home — would I ever see them again?

My brief, which I couldn't for one moment believe, was to undergo a four-week course in the Berber language? Not to reason why I presented myself to the language faculty at Oxford (just along from Beaumont Street) and met my tutor, an Algerian by the name of Hakim Haddad. French was easy to learn thanks to Mother, but this was so difficult as was the written word too, however I gave it my best shot on the basis B.S wouldn't have sent me there if not for good reason?

My four weeks flew by, and I have to say although it was a difficult language to master Hakim said I'd learned enough to "get by" which didn't fill me with much confidence. Home again and waiting for B.S's next instructions and somehow hoping they'd forgotten about me soon proved folly. They requested I go straight to Grendon Underwood to see the new base station set up (apparently the girls there would be doing the W/T's with agents in the field). Then to Bletchley Park for a two-day wireless refresher course and introduction to new equipment and from there to Buscot Park, near Faringdon for a refresher course and up-date on some new gadgets, but most importantly a briefing on my next assignment.

All of that done, and then came my final day at Buscot and my briefing began in the dining room where a Captain, a W/O and three men in civvies were standing around a huge table and with pleasantries over the W/O unrolled a huge map, "Well this is where you're going along with the new code name of Argon 989."

"That looks like Gibraltar?"

"Correct — it's crawling with spies and Spanish Nazi fascist sympathisers loyal to Franco and its haemorrhaging information, your brief is to uncover as much as you can about what's going on there, who the collaborators are, how the spy ring is operating etc, but be mindful of the fact we already have some agents there and the Royal Navy have their own intelligence operation on-going too. The navy will get you there and we have a safe house overlooking the harbour which will be your base. There is a British Consulate office which we know is watched 24/7, only go there as a last resort, the rest is up to you, any questions?"

"Why the course on the Berber language?"

"That will become evident sometime later!" For the next hour or so we trawled over the map with obvious questions, what's this? Where's that? etc until the briefing came to a natural ending with, "Get yourself to Plymouth then ASAP, and report to a Lieutenant Smithson R.M (Royal Marines) he will have all your new kit and will accompany you on the run down to Gib, it's a very dangerous place — good luck."

It was June 4th when we embarked Plymouth on a Destroyer en-route to join the Mediterranean fleet and an impressive four days later we slipped into Gibraltar at around 1100 hours for a three-hour lightening stop to take on supplies.

But while that was happening and with a naval ratings uniform on, I followed the Lieutenant across the dockyard to a small officers' accommodation block where once inside I handed back the uniform and donned my civvies, a quick check to make sure I had all my kit, a handshake from my chaperone along with instructions to leave at 0700 hours and mingle with the exiting nightshift locals and if I needed a one-way safe ticket out to report to the main gate and ask for the duty W/O.

"Oh, and here is the key to your new home, good luck."

Once more I was well and truly on my own again! Promptly at 0700 I made my way to the main gate with all my kit secreted about me. My new Webley pistol strapped to the inside of my right lower leg, my Fairbairn knife to the lower outside on my left one, bino's, tablets, silencer, silk map and the new "Steno Graph" micro-dot coded paper all stored safely and gripping tightly to my wireless case I mingled among the civilian nightshift on their way home without even so much as a cursory glance from the gate guards. Across the road and up the hill following signs for the Casino then right into the next road looking for Bay View apartments, through the front door up three flights of stairs to number fourteen.

My new home was small, compact even, with a sofa and a bed in the lounge, a kitchen with two ring gas cooker and a small bathroom with toilet and shower, it was adequate — just. The best part was the balcony with its brilliant view across the port and bay, in one corner a very comfortable looking cane chair was too tempting and about three hours later I woke from my welcome nap!

One of my concerns expressed at Grendon and Bletchley Park was the range of my new wireless set (an issue I came across in France) but I was assured the latest sets not only had more power but the newly created base stations provided a network of good reception across Europe and North Africa and everything was via coded Morse.

With nothing to go on I decided my only option was get out there and mingle, which I did, taking in all the side streets, stopping at bars and cafe's, buying provisions and just generally trying to be inquisitive without being conspicuous. Week one passed uneventful, the same with week two but one morning while walking along the fishing harbour a little van passed me which had a number ending 989, my number, I'm not sure why, but I watched it drive along the wharf side and stop some way ahead. The driver opened the rear doors and took three wooden crates out, the top one he covered with a cloth, next he went over to a fishing boat "The Magdalena" and spoke with the fishermen on board, then returning to the crates he carried the first one to the boat by which time I'd arrived and could see in the next crate what looked like a Lobster pot float, but it was slightly bigger than the others on the boat and of a slightly different colour but most noticeable was what looked like a telescopic antenna and at the opposite end a coil of about ten yards of wire with a foot-long canister attached, most odd.

During that night's planned W/T to base I mentioned the odd-looking pot floats but apart from that I had nothing much else to report. June was nearing her end when I heard the devastating news the 4th and 7th RTR's (my old regiment) had been all but wiped out by Rommel's Afrika corps at Tobruk and those who weren't killed were taken prisoner, my immediate thoughts were of my old crew mates. Such dreadful news.

Next night's W/Ts were more interesting to say the least, Bletchley thought the lobster pots were hydro-phonic microphones used to detect submarine activity. Base wanted to know if I had the name of the boat — I did, but my offer to further investigate the boat was met with a firm no, the navy will sort that, we want you to concentrate on finding the van that delivered them.

The only option was to search, street by street and on foot until eventually I spotted it being driven by the same man going along Rosia Road toward the bay. Making haste to follow it best I could on foot I eventually lost it but carried on in the general direction. It was twilight when I found it parked outside a small stone cottage standing alone near the headland and settling down to what I thought was going to be long night and mulling over what to do next the same man came out, got in the van and drove off.

The rear yard had a stone wall around it and assuming the house was empty I thought this was the obvious point of entry so over I went.

There was a workshop/store built into the stone wall which looked promising and unbelievably was left unlocked.

Inside it was crammed with all sorts of electronic equipment including more hydro-phonic floats, but more worrying was what looked like an S.O.E. wireless set? Then I heard the rear door of the house open and footsteps coming toward the workshop, the decision was simple, Fairbairn ready — a figure came through the door. As he did, I put my left hand over his mouth and rammed my knife hard into his chest, it didn't take long for him to die, but seeing him fold to the ground I realised this was not the man driving the van? Now I needed to know if there was anyone else in the house — only one way to find out. Pulling my Webley out and attaching the silencer as I walked across to the house, through the open rear door into a scullery area. When I heard the van draw up, decision made and with arms outstretched the moment the driver came through the door I felled him, one shot to the head, simple. Two down and thinking I'd already pushed my luck, I dashed back to the workshop and collected the S.O.E. wireless then got the hell out of it. Although Gib was only a small enclave it seemed to take me forever to get back to my room, but I did.

Still high on adrenalin I called base and using my code system relayed in Morse — van found, 2 down, have wireless set 1941-GB242. The reply — excellent.

It took me a few hours to come down, that and the heat kept me awake so I decided to make to the balcony and the cane chair, that did the trick until I was woken around 0630 by the sound of a distant explosion but couldn't see any evidence anywhere?

Still exhausted from the night before I decided to spend the day cleaning off my kit and resting on the balcony, until around 1800 hours when I ventured out for a cold beer (which was like nectar). There was some commotion and much arm waving among the local fishermen at the bar, asking the waiter why — he replied that a fishing boat had been lost, "They think it hit a mine blowing up and killing all on board."

"How terrible, was it a local boat?"

"Yes, the Magdalena!"

Back in my room and pondering once more on the night before and thinking how lucky I'd been so far, but also that luck wouldn't last forever. A fishing boat blown up killing three collaborators, one spy knifed and another shot suggests I must be top of their "find and stop at all cost" list. Mindful of that, I remembered the good practice door regime taught at Buscot, they supplied a simple wooden door stop to use every time one was inside. It wouldn't stop a determined break-in but it might buy some time? Also, the paper in the door trick. On the way out place a small piece of paper (or thread) between the door and the frame stop about three inches off the floor on the hinge side of the door poking out just enough to be seen, if it's on the floor when you come back you know someone's been inside! After a day's rest it was time to get back to work walking the streets again, but I didn't feel comfortable. Every vehicle that went by, every passer-by, cyclist and just about everything that moved was enough to panic me. At times I felt sick with anxiety and couldn't concentrate on anything. It was no good I couldn't carry on like this, so I decided to go back to my flat and rest up for a few days.

At the door I was relieved to see the tell-tale paper still in place, once inside and for the first time I jammed my door stop in place then went to my favourite place, the balcony. Sitting in the sun there I had this immense feeling of impending doom, a feeling of sheer vulnerability — but I knew I had to get to grips with myself.

I didn't venture out for the next two days and was beginning to overcome my anxiety and feelings of doom to the point where I thought one more good night and I'd be ready to face the world again, but no such luck! Something woke me.

I could see the door from my bed, it had a gap at the bottom through which I could see when the corridor light was on, but there was a shadow there, it moved very slowly then the door handle began to turn, the door was locked, chained and I had my wedge in place, I reached under my pillow for my Webley and with arms outstretched I was ready for whoever it was outside. The lock and the wedge were holding and clearly whoever it was didn't want to make any noise, slowly and quietly the handle began going back the other way until it stopped, next the shadow moved slowly away, as it did, I went out onto the balcony to see if I could spot anyone, but nothing, not even a cat. Needless to say, I didn't dare sleep and around 0100 hours I took one of my Benzedrine tablets. I stayed put until around mid-day and after having been vigilant all night and morning I thought it safe to go out, especially given I had no hard evidence to suggest it was a spy or local collaborator trying to get in, it may even have been a burglar.

Tooled up and with tell-tale paper in place I ventured out making my way north along Main Street toward the airfield where once there I sat for a while before heading toward the fishing wharf where I stopped again. Next, I walked back toward my flat stopping off at a small cafe for huge bowl of Paella. Leaving the cafe around 1830 hours for the ten-minute walk to my flat I was beginning to feel my old self again, albeit still very much awake from the tablet. At the door was my worst nightmare, the tell-tale paper was on the floor — someone had been in! Dilemma, were they still inside? Had it been booby trapped? Would they return? Did they see me coming back? etc etc. I knew I couldn't risk entering, equally I dare not risk going outside? Either way I couldn't stay by the door a moment longer, silently I went to the fire escape at the end of the corridor and undone the door to give the impression I'd left via it, hurrying back to the stairs (there was no lift) silently going down to the ground floor foyer area where I knew there was a store cupboard I could hide in for a while, which I did.

The cupboard door had an air grille in it which by bending one of the grilles slightly with my knife gave a wide enough gap for me to see most of the foyer and the glass entrance door. By now it was getting dark and the corridor lights came on and the effect of my tab was beginning to wear off, luckily, I had another which I popped and pretty much instantly felt refreshed again.

The hours ticked by, one after another, it must be midnight now and I was beginning to think I was overreacting, did I secure the tell-tale paper properly? Did the wind blow it adrift? So many thoughts going on in my head. Seriously thinking of leaving when I heard a car pull up outside, I couldn't see but heard two doors click open, shortly after two men, both carrying handguns came up the steps and through the front door — this was it, they were my assassins.

Peering through the grille I watched them quietly make toward the stairs, they disappeared from sight and in my mind, I was working out where they were, how near to my door they were? Heart pumping like hell and full of Benzedrine I felt invincible as I opened the cupboard door and made for the front door that they'd conveniently left wide open. I jumped down the five of six steps clearing all in one go, turning I could now see their car, lights out and engine running with the drivers arm out of the window. Decision. Poof, straight through his head, simple, now to get the hell out of here! Running like mad toward the sanctuary of the RN dock gates I guessed their silenced handguns would have a range of about fifty yards max so as long as I could keep that distance, I figured I'd be okay.

Clang! A bullet sped past my head and hit the steal shutter of a shop, they'd fired at me from my balcony, and they didn't just have pistols either! Now I was in it deep but just kept running and running toward the dock yard. Reaching the bottom of the hill and then left on to Rosia Road thinking I had less than a mile to go but very aware the road was pretty straight with no cover apart from a few parked vehicles I realised how exposed I was. Then with only a couple of hundred yards to go, simultaneously — crack — pain in shoulder — bastards got me, still running but waiting for the next bullet a volley of a dozen or so shots rang out from the direction of the main dock gate. Nearing the gate, I could see two sentries standing prone with rifles pointing skyward, one beckoned me through while the other fired off a few more rounds. Thankfully they were alerted by hearing the first shot from the flat, the noise of which carried in the still night air, they said they could hear me running toward them before they could see me, they then heard the second shot (the one that got me) at which point they decided to "let a few off".

By now all hell had let loose in the dock yard and a contingent of marines poured out of the gate and along the Rosia Road in search of my Nazi assassins. Meanwhile I was trying to see how badly I'd been hit, although it didn't feel too bad, but then again, I'd never been shot before and didn't know how it was meant to feel. Into the medic centre where they successfully removed the bullet. Fortunately, they were at the limit of their range so it hardly penetrated — lucky or what?

Two days later, I'm on a night flight Liberator of Coastal Command flying back to England when not long after take-off the pilot asked if I'd like to join him up front? The view was amazing, black as black could be below, but a million stars illuminating the sky above! Asking about our route he said, "We're tracking about twenty-five miles west of the Portuguese coast then slightly right into Biscay, toward Brest then we'll head out westward to cover the western approaches, then north again to cover the Bristol Channel, then swing inland to base, flight time around seven hours." Apparently it was quite routine and thankfully uneventful to but when we turned toward the Bristol Channel I spotted the North Star and immediately thought of Shepherd Grace and home thinking how on earth am I going to explain this?

Landing at Filton around 0400, the Liberator took on fuel for its return flight and I'd discovered to my relief Baker Street had laid on a car and driver to take me home. It was a Sunday morning and still too early to wake Pamela, so we went straight to Windy Ridge, just as well! Mother heard the car draw up and ran out of the house while Father appeared at the door. After all the usual hugs and tears along with mind my shoulder please I asked about Pamela which brought about an immediate silence. "Son, this is for you," said Father as he handed me an envelope, opening it, it read:

Dearest Sebastian, I could not put this into spoken words so I have written to you instead. In the past two years we have been in each other's company less than ten weeks, the rest of the time I have often cried myself to sleep not knowing where you are or if you will ever return and selfishly that was a situation I could no longer bear. It breaks my heart to tell you earlier this year I found another and now I am now carrying his child. My situation did not meet with approval in the village so I have moved far away.

Wishing you every happiness dearest Seb,
Pamela.

Taking a few minutes for this to sink in I began to realise just how de-humanised I had become, for sure I was upset, a little emotional even but probably a feeling of disappointment more than anything else. Composing myself I looked at my loyal and loving parents and said, "Oh well — in the words of the Shepherd, "Nothing lasts forever."

Chapter Nine

North Africa

Windy Ridge is a beautiful place and I can think of nowhere better to spend the summer months, but after a week or so there I was bored to tears and craving for some action again. B.S said I was to contact Buscot Park when (and if) I felt ready to go and with my shoulder almost perfect it was a temptation I couldn't resist, needless to say I was soon on my way there.

Into the dining room to be greeted by the same Captain and his W/O and the three wise men in suits my next operation was revealed. Another huge map was rolled out across the just as big a table, "There you are, Argon!"

Before me was a fairly well detailed map of North Africa, from Casablanca on the Atlantic coast to the left and stretching to Libya and beyond to the right, including the Mediterranean coast with all the major towns and ports. "Well, Argon now the USA have joined us as allies and Hitler has his hands full with the eastern front our attention is focusing on an invasion — the Germans are convinced we will do that along the French Mediterranean coast and we are doing are utmost to perpetuate those thoughts, however, the PM has convinced our new Allies that North Africa is the place to build a platform from which we can spring into Europe. At present most of the right side of this map is under Nazi control whereas the left is under the control of Petain and his Vichy collaborators, a difficult scenario made worse by the fact in 1940 Franco's Spanish army invaded north Morocco and declared Tangiers a Spanish enclave stating he was merely securing his country by temporarily occupying this "across" the water area, which in turn should have meant no Vichy or Nazis presence? However, Franco is under pressure from Hitler to allow Nazis troops to take Gibraltar, thus controlling shipping in and out of the Med, but that would bring Spain into the war as allies of the Nazis which in turn would lead to the Royal Navy annihilating most of Franco's ports, something he was desperate to avoid. To appease Hitler, he's allowed the Nazi's to build and operate a string of intelligence gathering stations along the Spanish coast and on the other side of the water in Morocco. To avoid detection by the Allies the Abwehr (Nazi Intelligence unit) are even given Spanish Military uniforms to wear. Trust no one, no one!

"However, we have an unexpected ally in the Sultan of Morocco — Sidi Mohammed. Angry at having to be subordinate in his own country to Petain and vehemently opposed to the Nazi treatment of Jews to the point of establishing his own Jewish refugee centres, he could become a significant player for us.

"But before any invasion can take place, we need more accurate and up-to-date information on troop movements, especially the Panzer units and that's where you come in again and why you learnt Berber, which along with French is the most widespread language along the French Maghreb.

"We need a string of communication bases, not sabotage units or the likes otherwise we'll be giving Franco an excuse to let the Nazis in, just reliable information from trusted operators. This is the list of proposed strategic sites where we need that info from, Casablanca, Rabat, Tangiers, then eastward into Algeria at Oran and Algeria city, but also south toward the desert towns of

Tafarooui and Constantine, both significant supply/reinforcement routes. Coastal Command will get you to Gib again and the Navy will get you to Casablanca — your thoughts please?"

"Supplies, how do I get them?"

"Two ways, air drop to desert locations identified by stenograph or by fishing boat."

"How long have I got?"

"We need as many as you can set up by November 1st."

"Better be off then?"

"Indeed, and grow a beard too. By the way there is a British/US collaboration doing the same thing, Massingham, steer well clear of them, this is singularly S.O.E. Good luck!"

Once more on a mighty Liberator but going the opposite way this time and in daylight! Apparently, we were to shadow a convoy of supply ships out of Liverpool en-route to somewhere in the Med, criss-crossing their route to Biscay looking out for U-Boats then handing over to another aircraft and continuing on our way to Gib. Landing at Gib with strict orders not to leave the dockyard I had a briefing about the run down to Casablanca which was to be that night in a Motor Torpedo Boat, (MTB) and then to rendezvous with a local fishing boat some miles off the coast of Cassa. At 2200 hours we left Gib for our rendezvous. I had all the usual kit under my tailor made Djellaba which unlike the traditional ones had inside pockets and slit in the side to reach my handgun. Sandals replaced shoes which meant my Fairbairn was way up my sleeve, one interesting addition to my standard kit of having an amount of local currency was a small quantity of diamonds in pouches hidden in pockets on the inside of my belt (although they didn't tell me how much in value they were worth). I carried my wireless set and had two more over my shoulder in a carpet bag. After an hour or so flat out in the MTB I was more than pleased to make our rendezvous, cross loading me and my kit took about two minutes then we pottered off toward the flickering lights of Cassa.

It was still dark when we pulled alongside the fishing wharf where we offloaded my kit on to a hand cart which Rahman (our skipper) soon got behind making off toward the town while beckoning me to follow, "Follow!" Soon we arrived at his house, a small very typical square building which at that moment in time and with nothing organised I had no idea I'd be staying in for a few days, but willingly accepting his invitation to do so I ventured in. He gave me a small upstairs room which was apparently his son's, but Rahman had evicted him to a store in the yard!

Once established in my room, it was time to go and explore, a melting pot of people the likes of which I'd never seen before, also there seemed to be a steady stream of refugees passing through? Looking, listening and trying to work out what was what I soon became aware my disguise had one major flaw? My legs and in particular my feet were lily white! Treading in every available mound of dirt and pile of camel s*** I could on the way back to Rahman's, I was quite pleased with the effect.

Rahman's wife had prepared a meal of stewed lamb (a dish I would become all too familiar with) and while talking over dinner it became clear Rahman had a strong dislike of the French and Germans, going on from that I asked about the refugees I'd seen earlier?

"Ah they are the Jews escaping from Vichy France and the Germans, there is a refugee camp on the outskirts of town, the Sultan provides them with food." Thinking that may be a good place to visit in the hope of recruiting my first operator I'd decided to go there next day.

The call to prayer woke me early and after a bowl of something resembling porridge I made off toward the refugee camp, but not before telling Rahman I may be away for a day or two? The camp was a very well organised affair, a large house almost palatial looking surrounded by rows of neatly organised tents with people coming and going in an orderly manner, mostly to and from a large tent next to the house, a good place to start? Once inside there were signs in German, French and Berber pointing to the "reception" desk which had a steady queue of mostly women and children.

An unexpected tap on the shoulder followed by "Yes you need help," spoken in a corruption of languages? I turned to find a determined looking young woman glaring at me. For once, I was lost for words, "Come." I followed without question into the house. "Why are you here? What do you want? Where are you from?" like a machine gun she fired off several questions at me to which I decided to reply in English.

"I am researching possible war crimes on behalf of the Red Cross."

"Huh — I can give you all you want to know about them, but why are you dressed like that, tell me your real purpose."

I detected an almost German twist to her English words. "I am incognito, disguised to avoid being detected. But where are you from?" I asked.

"I'm Jewish, from Austria, my family left when the Nazis annexed it and began the persecution, my father made it to England but my mother and myself were separated and made the journey here through France and Spain, we are hoping to get a ship to England one day, now you tell me why you are here?"

With nothing to lose (except my life) and with her obvious hate of all things German I decided to divulge some of why I was in North Africa and how I needed reliable contacts in Cassa, Rabat and Tangiers. The reply was music to my ears, "I can help you with this, we can establish your first wireless base here, we have experts here." Agreeing with enthusiasm I made off back to Rahman's to collect a wireless set. Returning that afternoon to discover she had already selected a possible operator who, in anticipation had made space in his tent and so I began to train my first recruit. I gave him (Michael) his code name (Atlas 1) the frequencies, stenograph, Morse book, sixty feet of aerial lead together with his call to base times. That done, and explained, we had some dummy runs which went very well, but I went on to express his role was merely one of reporting back on all German and Vichy activity, important too was to note the insignia on any uniform or cap from which a unit or regiment could be identified. He was very competent to the point I was satisfied he could operate without further guidance; however, I decided to stay overnight and monitor his next day report which was more than acceptable, good job done!

Making my way out of the compound the young lady came out of the house and gave me a piece of paper with the name and address of a contact in Rabat saying, "You can trust these totally."

"Thank you, but who should I say sent me?"

"Freud," she replied, "Just say Freud."

That evening back at Rahman's I asked the best way to get to Rabat. "The bus is good, it doesn't get stopped so you will be quite safe, it takes about two hours." After another meal of lamb, I bid the family good night and retired to my room to report back on my progress so far which was basically -Atlas1 established — Rabat tomorrow.

Next morning and I was on the bus to Rabat, nothing like the 22 to Wantage I thought, but it was interesting to see the hinterland and a level of poverty I never knew existed.

Early afternoon and we pulled into a very busy terminus, once off and making sure I still had everything I asked directions to the address the woman Freud had given me and around fifteen minutes later I arrived at quite a grand house (as things go here).

On the porch painted in bright yellow was the Jewish Star of David so I reckoned this was it. My knock brought a fairly elderly gentleman to the door, "Yes?"

"I come from the woman, Freud," was my reply.

"Come." As he turned, I couldn't help but notice his once expensive suit was now well worn and decidedly shabby looking, he asked, "Which of the Freud's did you see?"

"Oh, I didn't get her first name, dark haired confident and glamorous young lady."

"That would be Sophie."

"Who is she and why is she there?"

"They are related to a famous psychologist from Austria, most of the family fled from the Nazi persecution.

"Sophie and her mother Esti went to Paris, others to England and America, when the Nazis arrived in Paris the two women cycled all the way south and eventually crossed to here, they are well known and very much respected."

"That's some story, I had no idea although I did read some of Sigmund Freud's work at school."

"So what brings you here and how can I help you?" Explaining my mission again it was of little surprise to get the same response as the young woman Sophie Freud gave me and he went on to say he has the perfect person in mind to be my eyes and ears here!

"One moment please." And he disappeared upstairs returning a few minutes later with a middle-aged woman who he introduced to me as Ester. "Please, Ester will be your contact here, what do we need to do?"

Like a magician saying, "I just happen to have," I removed a wireless set from my bag asking, "When can I begin to train you, Ester?"

"After a meal, oh and you are welcome to stay here for as long as you like too."

Yet another meal of lamb, but this time in a Moroccan Tagine, a peculiar vessel with an upturned funnel for a lid, either way it was still lamb, but it was welcome and afterwards we got on with some tuition. Ester was very good; mind you there wasn't too much to take in. Next morning, we did some refresher work then satisfied with her capabilities I gave her the same brief as I gave Michael along with her contact time, frequency, Steno — map, code name (Atlas 2) etc and wishing her good luck I made for the bus terminal and Tangier!

On the bus and thinking how lucky I was to stumble across the young lady Freud and how that chance encounter has led to establishing two operatives in a week was incredible, I only hope the rest of the operation goes this well? The bus journey to Tangier with seven hours of bumps and bangs and side to side wobbles was far from pleasant, but like the previous journey from Cassa to Rabat it was uneventful. By the time I arrived in Tangier it was early evening, and hard to believe that just a few miles across the water was Gib, with a good pair of binos you could see the aerials we were transmitting too — ironic!

With no contacts here it was very much a case of treading carefully while I felt my way around, which I did for a few hours until the fading light, dictated I find a bed under the stars for the night, a grass strip opposite the Grand Hotel along with several other "way-wards" will do!

Using my set as a pillow (keeping it safe too) I soon picked out the North Star and for an instance thought of home, but only for an instance, I so wanted to sleep — and I did! Woken again by the call to prayer my first priority was to find a Souk (market) and food. Once fed and watered I was on my way again looking for the impossible, everyone, but everyone I viewed with suspicion, that's how bad it was. There were men in Spanish uniforms talking German, there were Spanish in Spanish uniforms talking Spanish, there were some Germans in Nazi uniforms talking German, there were men in European civvies talking French, Italian and even Russian, but no English was uttered, it was indeed a hopeless situation! The day passed on with no progress in finding a suitable place to stay and the thought of another night under the stars encouraged me to keep looking. Night time came and I was still walking the streets, so I made my way back to the grass outside the Grand again for another night under the stars. Another day began with waking to the call to prayer and thinking about where to go and what to do next in this pit of Vipers I decided to make my way down to the fishing port in the hope of having some success.

Like most fishing ports it was very busy, trucks coming and going as were fishing boats too and people everywhere.

Eventually I found a spot to sit and contemplate my situation, which was not good. Watching the boats arriving one caught my eye because it wasn't the usual blue and white, but green and red with a different port code too. Curiosity getting the better of me, I strolled over to where it had tied up and shouted to the skipper, "A good catch!" Or words to that effect.

"Yes, very good!" was the reply, but with a slightly different dialect.

"Where are you from?"

"Oran, Algeria," came the reply.

"Oh, what's it like there?"

"It's good — better than this shit hole and no Spanish or Nazi fascists either, you should go there!"

"By boat?" I asked.

"If you like, we leave after we've off loaded and on the next tide in about six hours, it will take us two days to get there, you can join us if you like, but you will work?" At last, a ray of hope.

Around mid-afternoon and I couldn't believe I was on a fishing boat bound for Oran, until about an hour out the skipper shouted to his two sons, "Nets!" and they set about casting the huge net out over the stern and there it stayed for an hour or so scooping up everything that entered it until the next order came, "Haul!" and that's when I found out what he meant by work! It was a good catch and once transferred into the hold the net was cast out again. Night fell and one of the sons prepared our evening meal (of fish) and while the other took over the helm I sat with the skipper keen to learn more of how and why he had such distaste for the Nazis, the Spaniards and to a lesser extent the French too. His hatred for the Nazis came about from their invasion of his country, he hated the Spanish because Franco collaborated with Hitler and they invaded Morocco and he hated the French because of the brutal way they treat the Indigenous Muslim Algerians, he didn't like any regime much, a true free spirit which I may be able to use.

Meal over, "Haul!" Time to haul in again by which time I'd begun to hear some mutterings of a conversation from the brothers who up until now had been virtually silent (one was Said the other Sami, twins as it happened) as we were hauling in, I said to both, "So you don't like the Nazis then?" With that Sami pulled a filleting knife from its sheath on his belt, revolved it around his fingers a few times then threw it with perfection across the deck — it hit the wheelhouse door point first where it bedded itself in about an inch!

"Nazis, eh!" Obviously, I'd hit upon a nerve.

As the day progressed, we cast and hauled several more times and I got the feeling the three fishermen were warming to me somewhat and this was confirmed when we moored up at Oran and skipper (Farid) asked If I would like to stay at his house — absolutely!

Once our catch was offloaded, we made our way through the streets of Oran to his house and first impressions was, he was right with his description, clean and cultured.

His house was modest yet comfortable, even having a room I could use for myself but most important it had electricity! Curiously there was no woman, no wife. But I didn't dare ask why. This time Said prepared the evening meal — of fish — but also some green vegetables and bread, it was good. As the evening progressed the three became more and more vocally hostile toward the Nazis to the point where I began to think something significant must have happened to them or their family, then out of the blue Farid asked, "Why are you here, even though you speak French and Berber you are not Berber, your skin is too pale." Now what?

"Farid, I am from England, soon you will have your country back, no more Nazis, no more Spanish and perhaps one day no more French too. But before that can happen the great force that will come here to free your country needs help."

"How can we give you that help? Not with our little boat."

"Of course not, we need information, information on Nazi troops and ships, how many and where, the buildings they use, where they store fuel, anything and everything they do we need to know about."

"We know these things, our family is big and spread across all Algeria — we are all members of the National Liberation Front — we will help you."

"Do you have contacts in the city Algeria?"

"Yes, many, my father and brother are there, they will help."

"Thank you, do any of you know Morse Code, do you use it at sea?"

"Yes, we know the Morse Code, for sea and to keep in contact with other NLF fighters".

Plugging the bare wires of my set into the wall socket I turned on, tuned in and sent my first W/T back in over a week. - location 3 blank — 4 and 5 good — need sets — air drop not poss — m t b — r v at sea. Some five minutes later came the reply — good with 4 and 5 — sets ok r v ok — w and w — need you back at 3 urgent — There followed a quick conversation with Farid to see if he was ok to R.V. with the M.T.B, if so where and when, he suggested about eight miles N.W of Oran the following night at 2200 hours from which I had a very quick look at my steno and gave an approximate position back, some minutes later the reply came confirming the R.V details. Excellent news.

Farid went on to say we would be making to Tangier from the R.V. not back to Oran.

Knowing I wouldn't be going back to Oran or ever possibly seeing Farid's father and brother to train them, I spent the next day going over and over operating details and instructions with Farid and his son's primarily so they could train the others.

Evening meal over and down to the boat, it was around 2000 hours when we cast off in the fading late September light. Slowly we made for the R.V. point until exactly two hours out Farid switched off and we began to quietly drift, no M.T.B. Ten or fifteen minutes passed and still no M.T.B, Farid checked and double checked his course and was sure we were at the right location, thirty minutes passed and we were getting ready to abandon the R.V. when Sami ordered, "Quiet! I can hear engines." Big Dilemma. Was it our M.T.B or French, Spanish or even Nazi? Should we have lit up or stayed silent?

Farid hit the start button and turned all the deck lights on, sure enough the sound of a powerful engine got closer, "Nets!" came the familiar order and the boys began to cast, we had about twenty yards of net gone when suddenly a blaze of lights fell upon us, but who from? Before we knew it the MTB had swung around and was along-side. "No time to hang about," came from someone on board her, "Spanish patrol boat around, that's why we're late, suspect its operated by Gerry's, hurry up." In less than a minute two large ammo type boxes were almost thrown over to us and the MTB disappeared into the dark. Farid, fearing we may be challenged at any time by the Spanish boat ordered we unpack and stow its contents immediately. Removing two sets from the first box Sami took them down into the fish hold while Said punched a hole in the bottom of the box then threw it overboard as I began opening the second box only to find one set and another box.

Opening that box, I found a quantity of P.E along with detonators and twelve grenades. Sami appeared and collected the next load to hide, and I told him to take great care with this box and under no circumstance must it get wet!

Said holed that box too and as with the previous one sent it to the bottom.

Goods safely stored we continued on our way toward Tangier until it became time to haul in, just as we were doing so, we were showered with light from a fast-approaching boat.

Before we knew it a Spanish Patrol boat was alongside. A search light swept across the decks and picked us out one by one as we were hauling in.

Next thing two heavily armed men, probably marines jumped on board and began searching around. Farid was brilliantly calm as he hollered for them to get off his boat while he was hauling, they took no notice and kept searching everywhere, Farid was screaming at them while we three kept hauling, but they didn't respond, they couldn't because they were Nazis in Spanish uniform! Finding nothing on deck and the hold hatch covered by the incoming net full of fish they jumped back onto the Patrol boat and sped way. A close call!

As darkness gave way to light Farid asked, "How long to stay in Tangier."

My reply was, "As long as I'm required,"

"Where will you stay?"

"No idea"

"I can arrange that for you." The remainder of the journey was going over and over operating instructions for the radio, he was Atlas 4 his family in Algeria was Atlas 5, I'd removed the Steno map and code book, the only kit with each set was a Morse book. Farid had noticed there were three sets, he asked about the third which I replied, "I was hoping to find and operator south of Algeria city but time has eclipsed me."

"We have good N.L.F contact near Tunis boarder."

"Oh, do you think your generator will power my set?"

"Yes." Opening up, bare wires in a socket and about thirty feet of Ariel lead run up the mast I attempted to call base, unbelievably the reply came back crystal clear, my message was Atlas 4 and 5 operational in 4 to 5 days' time, opportunity for Atlas 6 near Tunis boarder, proposed N.L.F operator not known

— ok to establish contact — the reply was brief and to the point — excellent 4 and 5 and yes 6, contact when you next can — "Okay, Farid, can you get the sets to the other two locations, I may be able to pay for your fuel."

"Sure, I can, currency is no good, worthless, can you pay in gold?"

"Leave that with me and I'll try to get you some for your next visit to Tangier."

It was midday when we tied up in Tangier and the fish man Farid used to take his catch to market was waiting dockside, Farid went ashore and the two had a conversation which by much arm gesturing at me suggested I was the topic.

Farid beckoned me ashore and introduced me to Khalil saying he is from Oran too and a member of N.L.F. you can stay with him — he will look after you.

Back on board to collect my belongings Farid asked for a few of the grenades, I gave him four on the condition they must not be used anywhere in Morocco, he agreed.

So, I was now in a fishmonger's van heading into Tangier thinking, 'One day I may be able to tell my parents about this, but they would never believe me!'

Chapter Ten

Paving the Way

Khalil was a softly spoken man, my first impression was he's more of a thinker than a fighter, but very polite and welcoming, his house was clean and tidy especially for a man living alone, but I later discovered his home was in Oran and he used this as a base for his work. He took me to a small cafe near the market for an evening meal (of fish) everyone, but everyone knew him and it was clear he was a very popular and useful man to befriend. That night I made contact with base and after explaining recent events to them the real reason they wanted me back here so quickly became evident.

It was the beginning of October, just a few weeks away from Operation Torch (the Allied Invasion of North Africa) there was growing evidence the Nazis had some sort of new device for detecting shipping at night from a base station somewhere along this stretch of coast, but it wasn't radar, it was new technology, and my mission was to locate it and either capture or destroy it.

Khalil's day began early with a trip to the fish wharf to pick-up the overnight catches, then to the market to sell, after that it would be late morning before he would load his van again this time to deliver orders to the restaurants, hotels, hospitals and some government buildings. Accepting his offer to ride with him was an opportunity too good to miss, seeing the city and all the important buildings, we even delivered to the German Embassy after which Khalil suggested we plant a bomb in a fish — we laughed about that all the way back to his house! Over dinner I explained to Khalil the theory about a Nazi spy device operating somewhere along the coast and my intention was to walk the coat lines looking for possible buildings and sites where this might be operating from. He suggested dropping me off at first light about fifteen miles west of Tangier for me to walk back — a good idea and next morning he did just that.

Leaving me at a very remote headland I began my walk back, the land was quite baron with the odd goat herders hut, but nothing of any significance, in fact the only place habitable was a small fishing village of about five or six tiny houses, even so the view they had of the Straights of Gib was mostly obscured by a large outcrop.

Mid-afternoon and I found myself looking down on the outskirts of Tangiers, I decided to sit and scan the buildings and skyline for a clue, but nothing, not even the German Embassy building had a window giving the correct line of vision.

That evening we discussed my search and agreed on searching fifteen miles to the east the following day and next morning Khalil dropped me off in a very similar environment as the day before from where I began my walk back to Tangier. More of the same mostly baron sandstone with the occasional animal track, but again nothing of any significance and by the afternoon I found myself on the outskirts of Tangiers again with nothing to show for my trek.

Walking through the town back to Khalil's I caught glimpse of two men in civvies who I thought I knew from somewhere, but before I could get a second glance they had vanished around the next corner, odd that.

Over dinner and pondering where to search next, I withdrew my silk escape map hidden in the lining of my robe and together with Khalil scoured it for possible sites and it wasn't long before we both came to the same conclusion. Tangiers was not the ideal location for this new piece of equipment, it was not the closest point to the Spanish Peninsular and viewing a straight line from Tangier to Gib was obscured by the headland to the east.

Mindful of that we decided the ideal location was from a spot about twenty miles further eastward and along the coast from there for about another thirty miles? In short, from Ksar-Es Seghir to Eddalya a distance of about fifteen or sixteen miles and then from there to Belyounech, another eight or nine miles, it had to be there surely. A call to base informing them of my intentions which thankfully was met with approval, then bed.

Before dawn we were up and away to Ksar leaving my set with Khalil but taking some smoked fish, cured lamb, some bread a chunk of cheese and my shoulder sack of water. The plan was that I would overnight somewhere and Khalil would pick me up the following evening from Belyounech. So began another trek across more barren landscape and although the coastline was rugged and beautiful, it was devoid of anything of interest.

Late afternoon and nothing, not even a herder although I had a clear view of the Spanish mainland and the huge rock that was Gib for most of the way until I dropped down into the small town of Eddalya, a peaceful little place oblivious to what was going on in the world around it. I decided to bed down alongside the only road into the place just in case of any suspicious traffic movements, but my night passed without interruption, nothing! Next morning, I chewed on my bits of fish and bread while following the coast line on my way to Belyounech and came across some vehicle tracks heavy enough to mark the sandstone.

Curiosity dictated I follow them toward the coast until the sandstone gave way to granite. Here there looked to be more evidence of recent activity and what looked like a well-trodden path going down to the sea, but also heavy grooves in the sandstone going the other way. Following the grooves for about seventy-five yards into a shallow dip I came across a sand camouflage net under which was a huge generator with an electricity cable running toward the sea. With no vehicles anywhere and nothing on my map to suggest anyone living here I decided to venture along the granite path zigzagging down toward the sea. Yes! About one hundred and fifty yards away was very obviously a freshly built block building, single storey, corrugated flat roof, a single entrance door with two "Spanish" guards, one of whom looked very much asleep. This must have been it, but I needed to see the side facing the sea. Quietly retracing my steps to where the vehicles had stopped, I made for further along the top to gain a view of the other side of the building which, as I suspected had a large wooden shutter, perhaps four feet by four feet that looked like it was easily detachable. This was it! Making my way to our rendezvous point just outside Belyounech I met with Khalil at the agreed time and with much excitement spoke of what I'd found, but that I really needed to stay overnight to see exactly what was going on there. We drove into the town and brought some food and water for sustenance during the coming night out then back to the R.V. point where Khalil dropped me off arranging to pick me up at first light.

By now it was around 2000 hours and the sun was beginning to set when sure enough a halftrack with two guards and three men in civvies came along heading in the direction of the target building. Once out of sight I made for the generator only to find they had already removed the net and fired the thing up! Next, I made for the spot on the rocks overlooking the building, the shutter was off and I could see a dim light inside. Shortly after something out of Dan Dare began protruding through the opening where the shutter had been, a large black tube with the circumference of about eighteen inches, is this their mystery weapon? Satisfied I'd found the location and I'd seen enough, my next priority was to inform base (without getting caught here) so I decided to withdraw back to the R.V. point and rested up until Khalil arrived next morning.

Just as the sun broke, my taxi arrived, Khalil was as excited about the discovery as I was, and all the way back to Tangier, we discussed what it might be and what we should do about it, explaining to Khalil that it was a matter for my base to decide on. As soon as we arrived at Khalil's house, he boiled some eggs while I got my set up and running, my message was brief, but to the point: located spotting device — on coast — easy target for RN — after a short pause the return message was — cannot be seen to be hostile — your call — my return was along the lines of — permission to engage — not surprisingly the return came back — granted — I turned to Khalil and said, "How the hell do we destroy that with only a hand gun and six grenades?" Khalil went into the next room and returned with a Bren Gun, but not one I was familiar with. "Where on earth did you get that?"

"From a dead German," he said with a smile!

"What is it?"

"A Beretta automatic?"

"Do you have magazines?"

"Plenty!"

We both agreed that we must destroy it ASAP, tonight in fact, but how? My Sandhurst teaching for such events was the three stages, 1, Identify target, 2, form a plan, 3, execute! Stage one done, now for stage two, We park up at Eddalya in the evening and under cover of darkness make for the location on foot, once there I make for the side of the building (I can get there without being seen by the guards if they're at the front of the building) exactly five minutes after we separate Khalil is to cut the electricity cable with a wooden handled axe, when the lights go out I throw two grenades through the opening into the building while Khalil covers the front door with his automatic. Easy!

The day went so slow, mostly because we were full of anticipation, eventually the time came for us to go. Now stage three. It was twilight when we parked up in Edda and after double checking our kit, we made off to the target. Finally reaching our start position just in under an hour. It was brilliant moonlight to the extent we could see the building clearly from quite a distance so much so we decided not to bother about watches and timing, as soon as Khalil saw me there, he'd cut the cable, the rest was luck!

"Ready?" he nodded and off I went like a church mouse, we could see there were no guards outside which made getting to the side of the building easy and once crouching down at the front corner I got two grenades out and removed the pins. Khalil saw this because almost simultaneously the lights went out, as they did, I stood up and tossed one in then the other. That was followed by shouts and screams from inside the building, then three or four seconds later there were two almighty bangs. Rubble and bits of roofing and timber began to rain down on me and still crouching I expected to hear Khalil sound off, but nothing.

Not surprising, I crawled out from under the debris to see nothing left other than the two front corners, one of which sheltered me. Khalil appeared and we stood in amazement and triumph at our work but heard a moaning, without hesitation Khalil let a burst off, but not a quick one, he emptied his magazine into the rubble spraying every inch, it was clear to see the hatred he was unleashing. The dust and smoke settled and we had a quick search to see if there was anything of interest amongst the rubble (apart from limbs, bits of flesh and bone) Miraculously, in what was the far corner under a pile of rubble, was a long wooden box, we retrieved it and once outside opened it to find another of the black tubes but lord knows what it was or how it worked, but I did see the name "Zeiss" on an I.D plate and I knew this company made scientific lenses. Placing it back in the box we decided to carry the thing with us, which wasn't easy.

We reckoned we had about twenty minutes before Gerry would arrive, and at speed we could get back to the van in about thirty or thirty-five max, as it transpired it took just under thirty to get to the outskirts of Edda. Worrying though, was the amount of military buzzing around, stopping vehicles and spot-checking people, this was not good. We made it to the van, box too, when a voice from an upstairs window whispered, "Khalil... Khalil."

"Yes," was his reply. Next thing, the door of the house opened and a figure beckoned us in. Khalil hugged the other man who was saying he heard the explosion then heard military vehicles going past his house, he went on to say, "It's not safe to travel for a while, stay here." Which we did until late afternoon before making back to Tangier. Not wishing to tempt fate we decided to leave our prize with Khalil's friend promising to return when it was safer. That night back at Khalil's I made a W/T to base with the simple message: target destroyed — device made by Zeiss captured — 5 killed — the reply was, — vital job well done — keep device safe — Torch imminent! After that we slept like babies.

Next day we went to the fishing wharf to meet up with Farid who was making his way from Oran with his catch. It was good to catch up and talk about our exploits and he asked about some gold (which I knew he would), "Sorry I couldn't get any, but I have these for you," and I gave him one of my pouches with four diamonds in. He was so pleased with them and gave me a hug. Once the catch was off-loaded, we shook hands, said our farewells and headed to market.

Thinking about the goods we left at Edda, we thought it safe to go back there in the afternoon. Approaching Eddalya all seemed quiet enough, in fact very quiet. Slowing down with the house in sight it was not looking good, the front door had been smashed to pieces with no sign of anyone inside, so we drove past and parked up further along. Khalil said to stay in the van while he investigated returning some minutes later with bad news. He was told a neighbour had informed the police of two strangers going into the house, they came, broke down the door, took Khalil's friend away and stripped the house. Apart from losing our box the worry now was if they interrogated him and he talked we could be next. On the way back Khalil suggested it was time we split up, and I agreed, it was late October, and I was aware the invasion was imminent so I made a final W/T to base from Khlail's while I could before we went our separate ways. — Zeiss retaken — informer active — fear being uncovered, the reply was clear — lay low — torch imminent — good luck. That done I hid my set under a slab in the back yard, shook hands with Khalil and left for destination unknown.

The grass strip outside the Grand Hotel beckoned and that's where I spent the night hoping and praying to see an armada of Allied ships in port when I woke, but no such luck. Thoughts of food took over so I headed to the Souk for some bread and fruit, not ideal but enough. Waiting to cross the road on my way back to the port my heart sank to my knees when an army lorry with guards in sped past followed by a staff car with my good friend Khalil in the back! He saw me but made no attempt to acknowledge me, thank God.

Thinking, 'Now I really needed to get away from here,' I walked back up through the market, hoping that might afford me some cover. Once there and trying to blend in as much as possible, I was trying to browse the stalls without showing my nervousness. I was looking at a stall of handmade glass and small mirrors when a reflection gave me my worst nightmare, I was being followed! I continued to browse while trying to get a better look at the man, he was not in any uniform and he appeared to be on his own, but not sure. Now what? Sandhurst tactics again. Identify? Yes, plan? He had to go, execute? Not sure yet.

I needed to be 100% about his intention so I carried on browsing taking every opportunity to glance back when I could, clearly though he wasn't very good. At the end of the market was the bus terminal. I'd already decided to get on one, any one just to see if he followed, I did and he did.

Walking to the back of the very full bus I sat on the seat just before the empty rear seat, leaving him that the only option. Off we went and I unclipped my Fairbairn, ten minutes or so we stop and half the passengers got off, on for a further ten minutes or so to the next stop and a few more got off, it was at this point I'd made my decision to take him. Off we went again for another ten minutes or so until we came to a stop, the end of the route. The remaining passengers got off as did the driver too. Knowing the bus was now empty I stood up to leave, so did he and with no touch lost I pulled my knife from my sleeve, turned putting my left hand over his mouth while pushing him back into his seat, stab — and push hard right into his chest, holding and holding until blood came through my fingers and he was gone, a quick look around confirmed the only person near was the driver who was sat on a bench engrossed reading a newspaper, quietly I made my exit and off, job done!

Now the cat was out of the bag and they knew my whereabouts, but my hope was pinned on the invasion, if I could just hide away, in a ditch even until the allies arrived then I knew I'd survive. It was late afternoon, I was hungry, on the run with no way of contacting any one, not good. I came across another small park with a few vagrants and decided to try and blend in there for the night, but with all the thoughts going on in my mind sleep was impossible. It must have been around 0300 hours when I first heard the sound of heavy artillery, not howitzers, this was ship gun fire, Operation Torch was underway. All "us vagrants" were standing up watching huge white flashes of gun fire coming from out at sea followed several seconds later by the whoosh of a shells passing overhead, then some seconds later explosions and more flashes, quite spectacular so much so I concluded whoever it is after me, Spanish or Nazis, they would have enough to contend with now without thinking about me so I decided to make my way slowly back to the port.

My first glimpse of the port was a sight to behold, American landing craft and troop carriers disgorging men, guns, tanks, jeeps, it just kept coming and out at see the U.S Navy were sending shell after shell over our heads way inland. Such a feeling of relief went through my mind that I thought it safe enough to venture down to the little cafe near the port. Once there I sat outside and watched the yanks doing their bit, jeep after jeep with all ranks were speeding by, tremendous stuff. The waiter came and I ordered a coffee while I carried on watching this spectacle unfold, but after a while I began to wonder where my coffee had got too. Turning to the cafe I saw he was just coming with my drink, but behind him were the two men I saw the other day who I thought looked familiar. I knew I'd seen them before somewhere.

With coffee delivered and the cup at my lips, a commotion erupted behind me, "Stop thief! Stop him! Stop him!" A young lad who had been stealing ran past me scattering chairs and tables as he went followed by the waiter who banged against my arm so hard my coffee was sent flying! Standing to see the chase I remember the sky spinning around and immense pain everywhere.

My next impressions were waking up, but where? I had pains everywhere and I couldn't see clearly, just a black and white blur, I could hear and I could definitely feel something in each arm. Checking furthermore, I found I couldn't move my fingers or my feet or toes, I could move my head and could see the hazy silhouette of someone, a woman, I think.

Yes, it was, she spoke in a soft American accent, "It's okay, you're okay." Next, what looked like a man appeared, "So what's a European man dressed as a Berber and carrying a Webley pistol with a knife up his sleeve with no papers doing in Tangiers?" My first thoughts were, 'I've been captured and they've drugged me before interrogation? What now? Sleep.' I feigned drowsiness and went back sleep. Not sure how many more hours passed and I had pretty much regained my sight, but still not all my feelings, deciding to wake I made some extra body movements to attract attention and the woman came back, this time clearly visible as an American Army nurse. She stood by my bed and I asked her how long had I been there and what was wrong with me? "Four days now and we think you've been bitten, a snake or a scorpion, a spider even."

"But surely, I would have felt that?"

"Well, you show all the symptoms of that, you were very lucky two medics were passing when you collapsed, you were having convulsions and had swallowed your tongue too."

At that point the man came back, evidently a U.S doctor, he said, "You're a very lucky guy, so who are you?"

Content I was at last in safe hands I said, "British Intelligence, I've been here for three months, sorry I'm so smelly." He laughed and assured me I'd be on my way home soon, "Will I recover my loss of feelings?" I asked.

"I hope so but I can't promise this type of poison is very unpredictable,"

"Poison? But you suggested snake or scorpion?"

"Venom from animals and poison have very similar symptoms."

"Could I have been deliberately poisoned?"

"Absolutely you could."

"Bastards, I knew those two at the cafe I'd seen before? They were the two who came after me at my apartment in Gib and then shot me in the back while I was making a run for it to the docks, they poisoned my coffee but thankfully I only had the smallest of sips!"

Chapter Eleven

Guinea Pig in Limbo

Ordinarily, the thought of a ten-day cruise from North Africa to England would be a chance not to be missed, but a hospital ship chugging along at twelve knots full of sick, wounded, the dying and the dead, in December and crossing Biscay was not a joy to behold, however, docking at Devonport on December the 20th certainly was!

Organised chaos springs to mind, at least that's what disembarkation looked like. Ambulances, staff cars, troop carriers, all in an orderly queue waiting patiently to pick up their cargo and deliver them to hospitals around the country, each of us clearly labelled with name, service number and hospital, all except me, my label had the letters P.D on it and nothing else?

Eventually I was at the front of the queue and unlike any other vehicle my "taxi" was all white, strange? Two stretcher bearers loaded me into the back and off we sped.

It was bitterly cold at the dock side, that and the fact I had no feeling at all in my fingers or toes made me feel pretty miserable and the nurse who accompanied me for the journey could sense that and tried her best to make light of the situation until I asked her where we were going, what did P.D. on my label stand for?

"Ah, well, you're going somewhere very special, Porton Down."

"Never heard of it what's it all about?"

"They specialise in tropical diseases, viruses, chemicals and poisons, it's nothing to worry about, honestly."

Once off loaded and into a very comfortable room of my own it wasn't too long before three doctors and a nurse came along and introduced themselves and more importantly their intentions.

"Welcome to Porton Down Biology department, I'm Paul Fildes, chief Microbiologist. We specialise in understanding nerve agents and the like, we know Mr Hitler has stockpiles of some very unpleasant chemicals in his arsenal like Sarin, Anthrax and Botulinum which he may at some point decide to use en masse, and to be prepared for that possibility we need know what we're dealing with. We believe you've been poisoned and we're anxious to find out, if we can, what was used on you, once we've established that we may be able to get you some feeling back, but to be honest that might not happen, just as long as you are aware of that?"

"Okay I understand."

"Good — settle in today and we'll begin in the morning by taking some blood from you and each day we want a sample of what comes out too, not pleasant I know but we need to know what's going on in that body of yours."

"Okay, is there a telephone I can use to let my parents know where I am, I've not spoken with them since summer."

"I'm sorry this establishment is so secret my wife doesn't even know where I work, bear with us for a week or so, please?"

So, my two weeks of being the P.D guinea pig had passed (including Christmas day) and the boffins there said they've have done what they can for me, which in short meant the cocktail of injections they administered, the daily pee and poo in a commode and the pints of blood they took appeared to have made little difference to me, yes, I had regained some feelings in my fingers and toes, but that may have just been my body healing itself, who knows? The good news was they brought a telephone on a trolley to my bedside and I was at last able to phone my parents. "Hello — see you tomorrow."

Arriving home, it was a wonderful sight to see my parents waiting anxiously at the door, I'd been away for six months during which time there were many moments when I thought I'd never see them again. But their smiling faces changed the moment I got out of the car and produced my crutches. Hobbling to the door, I could see that Mother was baffled as to why, with no apparent injuries I was on crutches, while Father had a look of curiosity more than anything else. Simultaneously they both asked, "What's happened to you, Sebastian?"

"Oh, they think I was bitten by a Scorpion or Spider, who knows?"

The next couple of months were probably the worst of my life, stuck at Windy Ridge in appalling weather, not being able to walk un-aided, even holding a knife and fork was impossible. Mother would cut my food up for me and I would stab it holding the fork in my palm with my thumb, often I recalled the words of the doctor in Tangiers who said I was lucky to be alive, but although I was alive, I was not living and the thought of having to be like this for the rest of my life was not going to be an option, that I'd made up my mind on!

Wilmslow came out to see me a couple of times asking if would like to work at Grendon as "wireless buddy" to S.O.E agents and although I know I could bring much to the table, so to speak, I saw myself as the poor relation, the one who they got, so I politely declined which was met with, "You know where I am?"

March brought about spring and some much-needed sun, Father took me by tractor to see the Shepherd who was flat out lambing. It was so good to meet up with him again, he's such an inspiration. His simple black and white view of the world and the people on it gave me just the right message at just the right time in my life, "Some may believe in God, others in fate, who knows, but nothing lasts forever and you're a long time dead."

One thing that had changed on the farm was that two of the hands who shared a cottage had been called up and in their place was a Chinese family from near-by Milton Camp (Milton Camp was an enclave of Chinese immigrant families who came here during WW1 to help with the war effort, but decided to stay on here rather than return to China) Mr and Mrs Fook were very humble people and their two children very disciplined and respectful too, little did I know just what impact Mrs Fook would have on my life.

Crossing the farmyard on crutches Mrs Fook uttered her first ever words to me which I barely understood, suffice to say she was endeavouring to ask about my condition which between us both and with much hand gesturing I think she eventually understood, or so I thought. She beckoned me to follow her to their cottage and once there a hefty bang on the door brought out Mr Fook. There then followed a cacophony of words exchanged between them the likes of which I've never heard of before after which Mr asked (in very broken English) what was wrong with me and in my best broken English back I did my utmost to explain what had happened. There then followed an even louder exchange between them after which Mr said, "She can fix you, come in house." With nothing to lose except a life I'd lost the value of, I followed and sat down in the kitchen (it was the first time I'd ever been in the house). Another exchange and Mr said,

"Tongue." Which I poked out and Mrs studied closely — next came hands — and Mrs studied my palms and oddly enough my finger nails — next feet — at which point Mrs got down and removed my shoes and socks and began to study the soles of my feet, then my toe nails, then a very long, "Aaaahhhh shen — shen — shen!" Then Mr said, "You have a problem with your kidneys, they not working fully, she can see that by your nails and tongue, she can make you better," which left me uttering under my breathe I doubt that very much!

Next morning and with an open mind I went to see Mrs F, cynically waiting for some type of dance to happen, but no. She gestured to me to remove my shirt which I just about managed, sit, I did, then she removed my shoes and socks and from a neatly rolled material she laid out in front of me about a dozen or so very thin but quite long needles! Without hesitation she stuck one into the top of my arm, (surprisingly with no pain) then another in the other arm, next the same between my first finger and thumb of both hands, then she turned her attention to my feet, a needle each near my heels, one each between my big and first toe and two each in the ball of each foot.

Pointing at the clock she said, "Sit." Which I gathered meant for about twenty minutes of being like a pin cushion. She disappeared into the kitchen for a short while then came back with a bowl of "stuff".

"Huang Qi."

"Pardon?"

"Huang Qi — good — good," so I foolishly drank it! The twenty minutes passed and she began to remove the needles, but interestingly, no blood. So, with her help my attire was re-attached and I hobbled home.

Expecting a miraculous recovery, I was disappointed to find

when I woke next morning, I was exactly the same, but unlike the Gestapo she didn't try to poison me so I decided to persevere with Mrs F. This regime continued for about nine or ten days until waking one morning I found not only had the pins and needles in my fingers significantly reduced, but that there were definitely some signs of movement. Could this be real? Of course it couldn't, could it?

By now April had arrived, the hedge rows were bursting, the Thrushes were singing and the Stags that roamed the downs freely were calling, a magical time of year at which point I was feeling much more positive about life, I'm not sure if it was down to Mrs Fook's needles and potions or my body healing itself in the course of time, either way the headaches that were sometime so severe they would bring me to tears had significantly reduced, not just in their strength but their frequency too. But most importantly apart from my first finger on my right hand (which randomly had a mind of its own) my hands and fingers were working well enough for me to button my shirt and tie my laces, amazingly too was the recovery of feelings in my feet and toes which with the exception of both big toes (they were still very painful) were also functioning reasonably well, however the leg cramps, particularly in my right leg were still causing me an amount of grief, especially at night when sometimes my calf muscle would completely distort into cramps, bringing with it immense pain.

By May I was still having my daily treatment from Mrs F but was well enough to drive my car again and that brought me a sense of not only having conquered the effects of the poison, but also the demons in my head. Throughout this time though our family doctor John Kendal was brilliant too and although he was not convinced about Mrs F's "quackery" he went along with the idea and with his medicine brought about much pain relief for me.

In the car, where to go? I knew I'd pay a visit to Wilmslow in Oxford — pressing that bell button again and the familiar voice asking the familiar questions I was soon ushered in to see him. His first words, "Bloody hell how the heck have you made such a recovery?" Trying to relay two months of ongoing Chinese treatment into a short sentence wasn't easy or convincing however he then asked the question I was praying he would, "Ready to come back to S.O.E then?"

"Do I need to answer that?" Excellent!

"Come on then, over to the Randolph to celebrate your recovery and return."

Clutching the first pint of bitter I'd had for months I was eager to know how the contacts I'd set up for Operation Torch had performed.

"Excellent," he replied, "Especially the Algerians, but the jewel in the crown was the contact near the Tunisian border. The night before Torch he sent word on the location of a forward supply dump the Allies new nothing about, two days later the R.A.F hit it, they say the explosion was heard twenty miles away! Oh, and that box you found and lost turned out to be an Infra-Red night vision device, the R.A.F hit the factory a few weeks later."

Chapter Twelve

Back in the Fold

Trying to explain to Mother that I was ready to return to the "Army" was beyond difficult until Father intervened, saying, "He may as well go, Mon — he's like a fish out of water here, besides he knows the ropes, he's a big boy and he can look after himself."

Eventually Mother came to terms with the idea and all was calm, Father asked, "What's the plan, son?"

"Apparently, I'm to go to a rehabilitation hospital somewhere in Buckinghamshire for a few weeks, then if all goes well to an assessment board, if that's good I'm to go to back to Scotland for training,"

"What do you mean back to Scotland?" asked father.

"Oh, it's just a place where I will have a few months of physio and training to get some muscle back and to build up my fitness, after that who knows!"

"Shall we take him to the pub, Mon?"

They did, and it was good to see some familiar faces again. Old man Denton bought me a pint and shook my hand repeating the news I'd already heard about Sam being a POW. It was a lovely evening and a good time had by all.

Next day while I was getting my things up together for my trip to Scotland Mr and Mrs Fook knocked the door, and Mr F asked if it were true I was going away, in which case I would need supplies of Huang Qi (the magic potion).

Mrs F then produced a very old Chinese book on plants and herbs pointing to a beautiful illustration of a delicate looking purple flowered plant, "Huang Qi," she kept repeating, "Huang Qi," I shouted to Mother for help, Mother looked at the picture, "Ah — one moment," she returned with her mother's book of wild flowers thumbing through until she said, "Found it — Astragalus — or Vetch, it grows alongside the fields here." Mr and Mrs F had their usual very vocal conversation after which Mr proclaimed, "Now you know the plant dig some roots up whenever you can, you must always have some of this with you, once a day boil a few pieces and drink the broth, if you cannot do that and you feel poorly then chew on some raw." Thanking them both for all their help Mother and I bid them goodbye and later walked the field at the back of us to search for some and believe it or not and much to our surprise we found several plants, enough to keep me going for a while at least.

Off to Buckinghamshire and my rehabilitation course. Three weeks of bending, stretching and pulling just about every bone and sinew in my body, after which I had my assessment which basically announced I was almost two stone overweight and unfit (however they didn't pick up on the fact although much improved, my fingers and toes were still giving me random problems). They concluded by saying a couple of months of a good training regime including a diet and much physical exercise would see me fit to re-join the Army. Using my new rail warrant I'm on my way back to Scotland, this time to Castle Achnacarry, a few miles north of Fort William. The sole purpose for me at this god forsaken place was to get fit and the Commando who was to be my mentor for the next few months was a man not to be taken lightly. Nicknamed Grizzly because he just kept coming at you. Grizzly was relentless and even though this was the height of summer, it rained almost every day, that and the midges made for a miserable existence coupled by the fact most of the routine I'd covered before during my last liaison here training with the Commandos. It wasn't easy but the weight was coming off and I began to feel fit again, and an almost daily swim across Loch Arkais (and back) really improved my leg strength and foot movements.

The diet was interesting, lots of protein, fish, meat etc but easy on the carbs (they even gave me dispensation to eat my Vetch). Come autumn I felt good, good enough to pass the Commando basic training course again (which even Grizzly was complimentary of by saying the course has a thirty percent dropout rate) then on my way back home, much to Mother's delight.

I had a meeting in Oxford with Wilmslow where he laid out Baker Streets plan for me which was to go back to France in early March ('44) and pick up where I'd left off, but with a bigger picture in mind. Although no firm date had been set (to my knowledge) the invasion was to take place sometime in the summer and my role was to prepare the resistance for that event. However, he stressed it was vital not to raise the slightest suspicion of an invasion, so no increased activity, but equally not to go too quiet either, he went on to say I would only be told what's what on a need-to-know basis, that way if I were to be captured and interrogated Gerry wouldn't find out any more than they probably already Knew — "Thank you!"

By now it was winter '43/4 and then next stage of my preparation for France began in earnest with a three-day course at Bletchley Park being brought up to date with the latest wireless sets which included, thankfully, more powerful battery packs. From B.P to Grendon where I spent most of the time there listening in to "airway traffic" from agents in the field. Listening first-hand to who was where and the escapades they were up to was akin to reading an adventure comic, except this was for real and at times very emotional, difficult to know how the wireless operators, mostly women, not only kept their nerve but sanity too. After Grendon, it was back to Beaulieu for a few weeks of familiarising myself with the new tricks and gadgets the boffins had come up with during my absence and so by the end of February I was "good to go". With that announcement came my new "French" identity: Albert Garandeau, aka Reynard, a travelling seed merchant working for an agricultural company in Lyon, I had business cards, a seed portfolio and an array of documentation as well as a national rail card.

March 3rd 1944 and back at the same Bedfordshire aerodrome I last departed to France from where I spent most of the day being briefed and one of the issues that they were keen on ramming home was the new "Kommando Order". The captain said after the commandos and your mates in the Maquis made such a mess of St Nazaire a furious Hitler issued this order, read it and be under no illusion:

All opponents captured by German troops in so-called Kommando operations in Europe or Africa whether in uniform or not, with or without weapons, are to be exterminated to the last man, all quarter is to be denied them, this order includes agent and saboteurs. It is strictly forbidden to hold them in custody or as a POW.

He went on to say, "In order to give you some degree of protection should you be unfortunate enough to get captured we have 'assigned' you to a regiment, The Northamptonshire Yeomanry will be your parent regiment, I'm sure you know it's a tank regiment so you should be at home with them, the Major on the ground will know of your existence too." Making my way to yet another Whitley bomber to find the same P.T. instructor waiting to lift my chute on and the same Captain offering a "toddy a-for-you-go" followed with the same words, "Good luck, old boy," Together with a hint of familiarity I boarded and off to France we went, apparently taking the same route as before. An hour or so after take-off the same, "Five minutes to drop off!" was announced.

Double checking I had everything, "Hatch open!" and while connecting up the static line, "Sixty seconds — thirty — twenty — Go!" Once more I was plummeting toward French soil but unlike my first "blind" drop this time I was to be met by my old comrade Raphael. My parachute instructor would have been proud of my landing and once up on my feet a soft flash lamp appeared aiming in my direction, immediate thoughts were Gerry or Raphael? Fortunately, the latter and after a quick hug and handshake we were making off on foot and at speed. Planning or good fortune had the drop location pretty much as close to Raphael's garage as the previous time, so it wasn't too long before we were back at his home where once warmed up we chatted about everything until the nervous energy that had kept us both awake had expired and we both "conked out" by the fire! Next day Raphael was eager to show me our new mode of transport he'd created, two cycles, each having a trailer, but the trailer was made into a chicken coup about two feet wide and four, long, cleverly he had created a hidden compartment under their floors just large enough for some weapons, ammo, grenades and even a radio set, under mine, brilliant! Raphael was also eager I should meet up with the Star Line operatives again, especially Orion (Nantes) and Vega (Bordeaux) and went on to say twenty-three Allied service men had successfully transited the line all the way to Spain including three commandos from the St Nazaire raid. The next few weeks was pretty much spent re-kindling old friendships and listening to the mischief they'd been creating. Early May and I was coordinating the first of many air drops to my friends as well as bringing them up to speed on the latest P.E, detonators and self-timers, one of which was with "Orion" when, much to their amusements, we used the latest kit to blow a rail viaduct near the Parc de National! Throughout May the R.A.F continued to support us with numerous air drops. Various guns, ammo, grenades, explosives and even the occasional Nazi uniform were all delivered with pin-point accuracy, so much so we didn't lose or miss a single drop, but more importantly we didn't lose any of our French friends either. Champing at the bit to be let loose with their fresh deliveries it was extremely difficult to stop the Maquis from having a field day, but they abided by my brief to the letter which was to be measured and hold back because their new stocks will be needed during the forthcoming invasion, an invasion they were convinced would be along the Mediterranean coast and I supported that by saying their kit would be needed to stop Nazi reinforcements coming from the North to the South — but in reality it was the other way around. During my W/T's to Grendon on June 1st, they issued a coded a list of strategic targets they wanted attending to, mostly rail junctions and bridges along with several road bridges too, but their main priority was the string of communication masts that stretched from the Brest peninsular all the way to Biarritz. With it came strict instructions not to demolish until instructed to which gave the Maquis time to reconnoitre and plan. W/T on the night of June 3rd was the best news, D — 2 prepare for dem dates. Excellent news and we were all buzzing with anticipation until next nights (4th) W/T simply said — D pp 1 day- weather — D

= 6 th — but that news did nothing to dampen our spirits. The evening of the 5th came with a flurry of W/T's the first around 1800hrs was simply — dem com masts immediate — (and that instruction would have been picked up by Orion and Vega too).

No sooner received Raphael was out of the door and on his bike, chicken trailer loaded with P.E, detonators, a few grenades and his new issue Sten gun. Then around 0200 began the noise of the most horrendous artillery action which by the sound could only be coming from a naval bombardment. This was it, at last the Allied armies were on their way to free all of Europe from Nazi tyranny. It was around 0330 when a beaming Raphael returned, "The mast? I asked.

"It is gone!" The morning of the sixth came and apart from the noise of battle being fought some miles away to the north and the sky being full of Allied aircraft (each displaying their black and white invasion stripes) not much was happening here, a few Nazi Army units were seen making their way north, but nothing of any significance. The 7th came and went but W/Ts of that night we were told units of the Waffen SS together with the 2nd Panzers were reported to be making their way northwards from the Mediterranean coast near Marseille, to reinforce the Normandy garrisons and must be delayed at all costs. I sent — Vega is nearest — the reply was one we didn't want to hear — Vega down — go south to stop asap —

Looking at the map we reckoned their journey north was about six hundred kilometres and even if they could cover one hundred to one hundred and twenty-five kilometres a day it would take them at least three days to get to us and another day to get to Normandy so we decided to drive as far south as we could until we located them, then work out a plan.

The morning of the 8th and we we'd loaded the van with

everything we could, including Raphael's bike and four chicken. Our plan was to get to Poitiers then make it up from there. Arriving at Poitiers late afternoon and knowing how "Tankies" don't like night travelling we decided to sleep in the van at a farm Raphael knew to be part of the Star Line. Then came the dreadful news from the farmer, Vega had been caught, rounded up after a Nazi hunt for the Maquis who demolished their communication masts, it was rumoured they were reported by a collaborator. The three were immediately hung in a square in the centre of Bordeaux. Raphael was devastated. The day of the 9th and we were off south again, clearly the news from Bordeaux had impacted on Raphael to the point where I became concerned for both our wellbeing and so I decided to go only a few Kms south then park up and wait for the convoy to reach us coming the other way, after which when they night stop, we would go around them to the north and blow the first bridges etc they would come to next day, we waited and waited, all day we waited, but still, they'd not arrive? The morning of the 10th and we decided to go further south for no more than twenty miles and if we hadn't come across them by then we must assume we're on the wrong route? About an hour into our journey and we could see smoke coming up about three or four kilometres away, knowing there was no actual conflict anywhere near we decided to park up somewhere out of sight and make for the direction on foot. Little did I know what I was about to witness would haunt me for the rest of my life!

Chapter Thirteen

Oradour-sur-Glane

With the van out of site, we made off toward the smoke which according to our map was from a village named Oradour-sur-Glane. We were tracking along tall hedgerow when a young boy, nine or ten came running toward us. Raphael put his arms out and wrestled the lad to the ground, clearly in a severe state of shock he was struggling to breathe and sobbing profusely between large gulps of air. Raphael wrapped his arms around him and brought him to his chest like a mother would a baby, eventually the boy calmed enough to say: "Tanks came this morning, they rounded up all the men to the square, a man in a tank shouted something in German and they shot all the men with their machine guns, my father, my uncle, every man in the village is dead," Raphael asked where the smoke was coming from. "I don't know, I was picking peas when they came — I saw them taking all the women and the children into the church — that's when I ran and ran — my mother and my young sister were taken into the church."

"Did you see the person who was giving orders?"

"Yes, he was in a tank with the number 819 and a skull picture painted on the side, please go and find my mother."

We couldn't leave the lad — he was beyond himself with grief and severe shock too so we took him back to the farm knowing they would take care of him. Making our way back along the hedgerows again we got to a point where we could see part of the village, there were guards along the road in and much activity still going on as we could hear the occasional shot ping off. Clearly too dangerous to attempt going in to the centre we decided to hide in the hedgerow until dark then go and see what's been going on. However, late afternoon we heard the sound of engines starting up then soon after we saw a column of tanks pulling out of the village, the lead tank was 819 and we could clearly see the skull on the side as the boy described. They were followed by a convoy of support trucks carrying Waffen SS soldiers and supplies. The logical thing would have been to withdraw and attempt to follow the convoy as we'd originally planned, but something horrendous must have happened in that village and we needed to know what.

On hands and knees and sometimes belly crawling we slowly edged our way along to a point where we had passed the guards on the outskirts of the village and reckoned we were about half way along it when the hedgerow became rear gardens to a row of houses. There was no one to be seen or heard anywhere, we spotted a half open back door, silently going over the stone wall we made for the door and quickly went inside. The house was empty but had clearly been occupied as there was the remnants of a meal on the table? Creeping upstairs in the hope of peeping from a bedroom window nothing could have prepared us for the sight before us — if ever there was a hell — this was it, we were looking across the main square where a pile, literally a pile of bodies lay, all male, old men young men, all ages laying there dead as dead can be, some with bloodied bodies some not, just dreadful, but worse was to come. We couldn't actually see where the smoke was coming from so we left the house and crept further along the row to almost the end house which we went in and upstairs to the front facing bedroom. I don't know if I will ever be able to covney in words what was before us. The church had been set alight and its roof had fallen in, outside in random places, were the bodies of women and girls.

Looking closer at the church we could see the charred remains of hundreds — hundreds of bodies contorted and twisted and smouldering, What in God's name had happened here? Whatever human being was capable of this? I looked around to Raphael, he had slid to his knees and was sobbing like a baby, he was inconsolable, devastated and broken beyond repair. I knew we had to get out of there, not just to save ourselves but to make sure the Lucifer who did this faces justice, and that was my pledge to myself — "I will hunt you down!"

Trying as much as possible to keep Raphael quiet we slowly made our retreat out of the house, over the wall and back along the hedgerow to the van where once inside I contemplated on what I'd witnessed while Raphael sat motionless with his head pressed against the side window. Now what?

For sure we had witnessed the worst any human could do, genocide even, but logic told me with Raphael in no fit state my only option was to try and head back to his place. We'd been travelling for about an hour or so and dusk was approaching, Raphael hadn't so much as uttered a word when way up in front I could see the tail end of the convoy, stationary. I stopped and got the map out, there appeared to be a turning to the right a few hundred yards before the convoy and realising this would be a good route back being away from the coast, I opted for it. Starting off again Raphael came to life, he'd spotted the convoy too and as I turned right at the junction, he told me to stop, I said that it was too dangerous, next thing he pulled out his hand gun and pointing it at me said, "This is my destiny, stop or I shoot you."

So I did. He was quite mad, insane, his eyes were glazed and he was grey in colour and I was not about to try and stop him. He got his bike and trailer out of the van and rode off toward the parked trucks. Instinctively I knew he wouldn't be coming back. He passed a few trucks then pulled in between two and out of my sight. Opposite was a Tabac with several Nazis seated outside drinking and eating, next thing Raphael appeared from behind the truck and threw two grenades into them, no sooner had they gone off he began to open up with his Sten gun. He was standing in the middle of the road unloading his weapon into the dead and injured Nazis, he stood for less than a minute before he was cut to ribbons.

The situation was hopeless, an hour ago I witnessed something I never thought mankind capable of and now my best friend and comrade had been mown down. Realising too all the detonators for the P.E. I'd hidden in the van were in Raphael's trailer had put paid to any demolition work I could do so it was time to get the hell out of there.

Driving east for about fifteen kilometres I knew I needed to be heading North at the next opportunity which wasn't too long coming. Another hour or so and its well into the night when I decided to stop for a while, clear my head and take stock of the map as to where I was (which incredibly was about twenty-five kilometres south of my Grand Parents farm). Chewing on some dried vetch which I'd stowed in the van and taking in much needed water I felt well enough to continue my journey.

Nearing their farm, I contemplated knocking them up and, tempting as it was, I considered it too risky to place them in such jeopardy by having an agent in their home. Onward North and passing the turn to their farm I was about fifteen or twenty kilometres from Raphael's when daylight came and another hour before I arrived at my dead friend's home.

Exhausted, bewildered and wondering what the hell this war would throw at me next, I decided to report back (if I could) what the past twenty-four hours had thrown at me.

Out with my wireless I tapped this: — register war crime — oradour -sur- glane — waffen SS + 2nd panzer m gun 100 + males — burned to death hundreds women + children in church — pole lost — It was some while before the message back came — war crime filed — pole lost — are you referring to agent — my reply was simple — yes — the reply back was without compassion — leave location — head 2 argentan — r v with jedburgh. Hummm.

Chapter Fourteen

Making For Paris

Jedburgh was something I didn't want to get involved in, they were three-man teams, in uniform, made up of one American, one French and one British, all intelligence officers who were parachuted in just after D-Day. Their mission was the same as mine, to make contact with the resistance and to organise sabotage and mayhem. In theory this may seem a good idea, but my experience suggested the more people involved the less secure you are. Although I had good info from B.S my more accurate info came by way of friends on the ground, the resistance and the allied sympathisers who were running the escape lines.

By now it was mid-June and nervous talk among the Maquis was W/Ts via S.O.E agents had some serious security issues? Many of its members had been arrested and were being interrogated, supply drops were being intercepted by the SS and the Maquis and Milice (Milice being Marshall Petain's Vichy Militia) were at war — French fighting French and with betrayal and collaboration rife was also enough to convince me the last W/T I received was false. Indeed, why drop agents (Jedburgh's) in the middle of a war zone (and tell me to meet them there) when just a few miles away are much safer drop locations? That last W/T was not from B.S. — they were onto me!

Staying at Raphael's was not an option, I had to move on. I

had decided not to make any more use of my wireless because I wasn't sure who was tapping out the Morse the other end, but before I smashed it to pieces, I sent one more message. — eta argentan 3 days — W/T on arrival — having no intention of going there might buy me some time. While in the garage siphoning the last drop of petrol from two cars there and loading the van with everything of use, including my bike and trailer, a large saloon drew onto the forecourt and four men sprang out — luckily, I recognised them as Maquis from the Bayeux area, they said they were going further south determined to find the 2nd Panzers and the men that killed Raphael, they went on to say every Maquis group in Western France is seeking revenge for his death! We had a brief discussion about the fact more and more Maquis and S.O.E were being uncovered and agreed there was some serious infiltration!

For me going south to Vichy France was out, going north would be directly into the Normandy battle area so I decided to head for Paris, but wondering just how much the SS knew about me made me nervous about using the van — the bike was my only option. I estimate the journey to Paris was about two hundred kilometres and, thinking I can do twenty-five kilometres a day suggested eight or nine days to get there, but if I went via Le-Mans it could have been possible to take the train from there. That was my plan!

After stripping everything of use back out of the van and hiding it around Raphael's I locked up and set off on a seventy-kilometre route to Le-Mans feeling incredibly vulnerable, no wireless or grenades and nothing pre-arranged, just my Fairburn to keep me company. After peddling like mad for about six hours I arrived at Le-Mans station surprised and relieved that it was a completely unchallenged and without incident journey.

"Single ticket to Paris please?"

The woman at the counter simply replied, "Papers." To which I produced my I.D papers and rail card — "One moment," My heart began to race, "The train to Paris is there but it is waiting for an attachment of German soldiers from the front given a forty-eight-hour pass to Paris. May I suggest you go by bus to Orleans then by rail to Paris from there, it will be more comfortable for you, the bus will be here in one hour." Explaining I needed to get to Paris as soon as possible she quite adamantly insisted I go via bus to Orleans, no ticket! An hour later and I was on the bus to Orleans, not many on it and hardly a German in sight except for the occasional troop lorry heading to Normandy.

Getting off the bus at Orleans I bumped into a lady walking in the opposite direction, but on reflection she bumped into me, "So sorry — silly me!" she said.

"That's okay — my fault entirely," and we engaged in some rather odd, rather pointless small talk. "Where are you going?"

"Paris."

"Not with those papers."

"What do you mean?"

"Your rail card has a spelling mistake on it."

"What?"

"It's okay, the ticket person telephoned me — follow me, but from a distance not by my side."

Entering a modest house on the outskirts of town and wondering if this was a Gestapo trap, the woman introduced herself as Nadine and said they'd guessed I was an S.O.E agent. Cautiously I decided to reveal some bits of my time in France and about Raphael. Surprisingly she said she's heard about Raphael's death and how the Maquis are taking on the Panzers that did it, she laughed saying the Panzers were now six days into their three-day journey to Normandy, such was the determination of the Maquis to wipe them out!

She went on to say she was the wireless operator and courier for the Historian group operating there and invited me to stay the night and continue my journey in the morning. Nadine went on to ask where my wireless and kit were, I explained how I thought I may have been compromised and hid everything at Raphael's, including my wireless before heading for Paris, her response was I couldn't go to Paris without a wireless and weapons, she would organise a drop of new kit for me and said I should stay there until it arrives. Later in the day she invited me to listen in as she made a W/T to B.S and top of her agenda was to tell "Reynard" I had made it to her company and requested fresh kit, that news was greeted with much suspicion by B.S and there then followed a string of security questions known only to me (including my chosen miss-spelt word) but I could sense B.S were not convinced it was me and would not commit to a supply drop.

This conversation continued over the next three or four days until Nadine finally convinced B.S. that I was the real thing and a drop was made. As we excitedly went through my new possessions which included a new Paraset (an amazingly small wireless) Nadine revealed she had already received instructions on who and where to move me on to! Now I could operate again!

Taking the train to Paris was decided to be too risky, the alternative? At 0400 hours, "The chicken man," he makes his twice a week trip to one of the markets in Paris to sell his "Rotisserie" cooked birds, if ever he got stopped the offer of a freshly cooked chicken worked wonders. Arriving in the Meudon district of Paris he dropped me off on a street corner where a few minutes later my chaperon appeared to take me to a safe house, a typical five story Parisian house set in a long terrace of similar buildings and needless to say my "room" had been carefully built into the attic behind a false wall (although there was a small window in the main part).

By now it was mid-July and there was an uneasy feeling here, the Parisians could sense liberation was imminent, but they were measured with their anticipation. By contrast, the Nazi's were nervous, trigger happy and full of suspicion. Random stops were being carried out throughout the capital, houses were being raided by the hour and any one the Gestapo selected was "taken away". Euphoria began to emerge one afternoon when, in broad daylight an R.A.F Mosquito appeared from nowhere and carried out a leaflet drop.

The message aimed at civilians gave locations the allies had selected for bombing and asked them to vacate those areas, they did and the following night the bombs fell. Two days later and another leaflet drop this time saying 'The Liberation of Paris is coming, to avoid injury or death please stay off the streets, listen to your radio, freedom is near, don't die now!'

It was the first week in August when instructions were given to the Maquis in Paris and the surrounding districts to prepare for an uprising prior to Liberation. Word got out and the French tricolour began to appear. It was around the 10th/11th the sound of distant artillery could be heard which was greeted with a mixture of anticipation and fear. Nazi infantry units and artillery began to appear driving through the capital moving northward, in retreat?

The radios and more leaflet drops were calling for civilians to stay indoors, which they did and in one of my twice weekly W/T's back to B.S I had instructions to go to the Port d'Orleans area and wait for 30 A.U to arrive (30 Assault Unit was a small, all service intelligence gathering unit of fearless hooligans). Then around the 15th from nowhere the Maquis began appearing on the streets. Barricades were built, brazen and fearless they stood their ground and took on the Nazis, street by street with their snipers picking off any Nazis unfortunate to be in their sights. As arranged, I was at the Port d'Orleans when General Leclerc and his free French Armoured Division along with his army of Maquis appeared en route to the centre of Paris, but closely followed by a small convoy of British machine gun carrying jeeps and halftracks, 30 A.U? They were expecting me and me them, just a quick wave brought one to a stop, "Woolforce?"

"Hop in." Apparently, Leclerc had disobeyed orders not to motor into the capital until the U.S army caught up next day — Liberation apparent!

30 A.U was tasked with collecting (by any means) as much intelligence and documentation as possible before the Allied forces proper arrived next day. Asking the sergeant what the plan was he replied: "We're on our way to the residence of Admiral Karl Donitz in some sprawling chateau," I asked why the hell was I there. "French mate, you're supposed to speak French."

"But he's German?"

"Yep — funny that." 30 A.U blitzed the place and took umpteen POWs (Donitz had long gone) while myself and some others got to grips with going through pile upon pile of doc's and papers only interrupted every now and then by the shout, "Cover!" followed by an almighty bang and another safe door was blown open.

Clearly though there was too much "stuff" here to even begin to sift through so the decision was made to remove everything we could. By morning there was a huge pile of paperwork covering just about every subject possible stacked in the hallway waiting for collection. 30 A.U had secured the Château by the time some infantry lads arrived, and we were off again.

Patton and his tanks were on the Champs-Elysées and the Parisians were going wild. But then came the reprisals, I witnessed several women in various states of undress, with heads shaven being bullied and taunted through the streets for "fraternising" with the Nazis and on one lamp post hung the body of Cafe` owner. An outpouring of anger after five years of occupation was inevitable. I stayed with 30 A.U for a few more days searching various Gestapo offices looking for anything of interest including evidence of the forced mass movement of civilians.

By coincidence I recognised a couple of the lads from my time in Scotland, (we joked about "Grizzly" not being here) and I asked if they'd come across the 2nd Panzer tank unit of the Waffen SS?

"Oh yes, mate, they took a hell of pounding at Caen when the Northamptonshire tankies took them on, their commander Diekman was killed then we chased them through to Falaise and pretty much finished them off there." That news left me wondering if the Tiger 819 and its crew copped it or not?

It was the last day of August (or even the 1st of September?) when I received new instructions — make for holland-location tba-: Bidding farewell to my new found pals of 30 A.U.

I jokingly asked, "How do I get the other-side of the enemy now?"

S.M Jacobs overheard me and said, "We'll get you as far as we can tonight!"

Chapter Fifteen

Onward to Holland

Dusk was falling and they were still celebrating in Paris when my jeep courtesy of 30 A.U, departed the city. B.S. instructions were to make contact with resistance in Reims where there would be a courier to rendezvous with at a location about fifteen kilometres northeast of Paris, so that's where we headed. To say the driver had a death wish would be an understatement but despite him trying to kill us all we made it to the R.V. point in good time. It was around midnight and not a soul about, "You sure you got your f***ing coordinates right?" Quietly enquired the sergeant.

"Yes, pretty much so."

"Well, we're not hanging around any longer, best you get out then." Which on reflection was understandable as we were probably behind the lines. So there I was again, on my own in the middle of nowhere in civvies with only my knife, revolver and radio for company, but confident my position was spot on, I decided to sit tight for a few hours.

Daylight arrived but sadly my couriers didn't and I'm guessing they'd been intercepted somehow? It was September 1944 and the might of the fast-diminishing German army was in retreat toward the Fatherland, anywhere much more than forty miles north of Paris and the same amount to the east was an impenetrable mass of German war machine and local resistance groups were falling like flies, how the hell I was supposed to get to Arnhem was beyond me? Beginning my walk "somewhere" I could hear a vehicle approaching, it was coming from the direction of where I'd just come from, so I was hoping it was friendly, sure enough, a U.S jeep appeared with four GIs aboard, I stepped out and they pulled up alongside. "Hello, British Intelligence."

"Ha, ha, where's your bowler hat and umbrella then?" This was followed by much jovial micky taking while I endeavoured to explain my circumstances and they theirs which was they were an advanced recce unit trying to establish where the Nazi's were. That chance meeting proved useful though, I stayed with them for four or five days heading back to their H.Q. Each night and out again in the morning while not only establishing where Gerry was but to also find a location from where I could move forward. However, from my perspective the situation was hopeless, try as I did, I just couldn't make any forward progress.

Toward the end of September, Operation Market Garden took place, the idea was to have a mass para drop in Holland, overpower and capture the bulk of the Nazis army and bring about an end to the war, but in reality, it was an almighty cock-up. Thousands of Allies were either killed or captured and nothing achieved, more frustrating was the fact I was still stuck in Belgium! Over to the east, Hitler had ordered a massive tank advance through the Ardennes in the hope of breaking out and taking back Antwerp, needless to say the Allies threw everything we had at stopping that, tanks, artillery and infantry were all directed that way which gave a bit of breathing space in the direction I wanted to go, but it was slow going not made easier by the resistance complete lack of trust, however, slowly I made my way northward.

Early December came, as did new instructions from B.S

wanting me to make for the area in or near the town of Xanten close to the Rhine. Fortunately, by now I'd made contact with Belgium resistance and after spending several weeks being passed from one safe house to another I'd crossed into Holland and it was then I came across another U.S recce unit and after a similar exchange of small talk and pleasantries I jumped in the back and we headed very cautiously northward.

The GIs were saying they believe there are some Panzer Tigers up front that broke through from the Ardennes and are heading toward Nijmegen in order to cross the Rhine again. We'd covered maybe fifteen miles or so and the GIs were getting very edgy, but so far so good no sign of Gerry — which was odd.

Then one GI. suggested they wouldn't be using the highway's anyway, so we turned off and took to the country lanes instead. We hadn't gone far before we came to small village (Melderslo) which was exceptionally quiet, even in battle you often saw locals flitting about, but here not a soul to be seen. We gingerly edged forward further into the village until turning a corner toward the centre there they were!

Halfway along the main street two Tiger tanks parked up, one was crewed and about to leave, just as it did the crew of the second Tiger came running out of a house and clambered aboard as the first pulled away revealing the number 819 on the second tank, visible too was the skull and cross bones. This was the bastard responsible for the genocide at Oradour-sur-Glane!

"Follow them, follow them," I pleaded with the GIs but understandably they were having none of it so we drove up to the house they came out of and I went in leaving the GIs in their jeep ready for a quick get-away if needed. I went in — I came back out — I stood motionless for a while and as one the GIs came over I just gestured to him to go inside, he came out ashen faced and immediately threw up! Composing myself as best I could I went back in while trying to tell myself this was not some sort of an evil dream. There was a man, tied to a chair, mouth as open as it could be, eyes glazed and fixed — but he was alive, opposite was his wife, she was tied to a chair, her throat had been cut and her clothes ripped but on the floor between them was their daughter, perhaps fourteen or fifteen, her clothes were torn and she had been brutally raped then disposed of with a single shot to her forehead.

Going back outside, I asked the sergeant to get a medic there ASAP, and to log this as a war crime scene, also asking that they send a photographer to record what happened. He did just that but worried we were to near the enemy he said they were now turning back to H.Q. I said, "I can't leave the man inside like that," and insisted they go back without me, which they did.

Going back into the house I cut the man's wrists free, then went upstairs to find some blankets which I then covered the two ladies with. Despite my best encouragement and broken Flemish plea to get him to move to another room he refused, understandably I suppose.

There were some provisions in the kitchen, so I made us both a hot drink which he did manage a few sips of, it was going to be a very, very, long night!

The following morning the man knelt down by his daughter, near to her was the spent bullet case, he picked it up and gave it me, I have to admit to being close to tears when the U.S. sergeant returned with a field ambulance and a photographer, realising I could do no more I bade them all farewell, the sergeant asked me where was I going. "To find a tank," was my reply — I didn't look back!

So, I began walking north again knowing that Gerry, far from giving up was not too distant either. Later in the day I could hear the unmistakable sound of tank tracks on tarmac, sure enough a column of U.S Sherman tanks came into view then trundled past me en-route to Nijmegen, which was about thirty miles away. The Nazis had dug well in along both sides of the Rhine knowing an Allied crossing was imminent they'd wired all the bridges too. This was going to be their last stand and one hell of a battle was about to unfold.

I hadn't got very far that day — I felt absolutely shattered, nervous exhaustion I guess, oh for a mouthful of Vetch. Having witnessed the U.S tanks moving forward the Dutch began taking to the streets. One elderly couple who somehow knew I wasn't local invited me into their house, an invitation I gladly accepted.

The Dutch were desperately short of food, despite that, they found me some cake and cheese which was duly consumed. In our brief conversation even using my best French accent they'd figured out I was British which at this point in time was okay until they asked why I wasn't in uniform. Tricky now — if I told them what I do I would risk being handed over, but then again who to? "Spion, British Spion," the old lady said, which I'd translated to mean Spy and I couldn't really argue with that so I smiled in agreement and that brought out a bottle of Cognac, which I was ordered to sample.

We managed to engage in much conversation, to the point where they insisted I stayed there overnight. Later that evening (and in hindsight stupidly) I fired up my wireless and called up B.S. for an up-date — *objective xanten-report enemy assets asap-* with no map I translated the Morse to my hosts who produced a map and with pointed fingers strongly spoke, "Nazis, Nazis!" which I took to mean it's still heavily occupied.

The gentleman succeeded in explaining on the map the fact between here and Xanten was the river Meuse to cross, but more importantly a narrow strip this side of the river was still occupied and the other side was the German front line, no sooner said and the Dutchman was out of the door uttering "Moment, moment."

Sometime later he returned with a man who apart from speaking English introduced himself as the Dutch man's son. "I can get you to the river tomorrow night, but it will be very dangerous, we have to pick our way through the Germans who are garrisoned all the way up to Nijmegen, but it can be done."

"Good but how do I cross the river?"

"I will arrange for a rowing boat, but you will have to cross yourself."

"Sounds like a bit of a plan then!"

Next day I did practically nothing apart from one brief W/T to B.S giving them an update but the rest of the time was spent looking out of the window, waiting and watching. The only thing of interest was a convoy of about ten or twelve British jeeps heading north and judging by their very un-army like appearance I guessed they were either SAS or Commandos?

Around 1700 hours my hosts gave me a meal of potato and fish, all they had I think and realising I still had several hundred dollars scattered about me I gave them a small wad, probably a hundred dollars or so, they were overjoyed but we soon realised the seriousness of the situation when their son knocked the door. "Ready." With a quick hug of my hosts off we drove, apparently as far as we can go before getting to the Nazis front line which took about twenty minutes of very careful driving.

It was a bitterly cold night with a ring around the moon when we began the most difficult part of the journey on foot, but my guide had clearly done this before because at times we were so close to the enemy I could hear them talking and see them sat around small fires trying to keep warm. After an hour or so of the most intense concentration on foot I'd ever done we arrived at the riverbank, then going just a short way along the bank was the rowing boat. My guide (I never did know his name) suggested staying close to the bank for about four hundred meters to where the river narrows and takes a left turn, cross directly there, "Do not drift further downstream, it must be there." A shake of the hands and he silently disappeared.

Once in the boat, I did exactly as instructed, four-hundred meters, cross here, row fast and quietly, I did.

The almost full moon I didn't bargain for, I knew I must be a good silhouette, but it didn't take long to reach the other side. Pulling the boat ashore like a church mouse I was off loading my kit when from the undergrowth came. "Here — here." Thinking, if they were German I would already have been shot, I ventured to where the call came from when two armed men appeared. Clearly, they were Dutch resistance, they signalled with their fingers vertical across their mouths, "Shhh shhh," then off we went toward Xanten — I hoped.

Judging by the position of the moon, I guessed it was around midnight which gave us about six hours of darkness, but this was something else. Again, the guides must have done this many times before because time after time, we came across encampments so close we could even see them lighting cigarettes. After about two hours they whispered that we'd crossed two German lines now we had to make greater progress. By the time sun came up we'd just circled the town of Weeze where we met up with two more couriers who would take me the rest of the way.

Thankfully my new friends had brought a hot drink and some bread with sausage which was much appreciated. The next part was to make for the town of Udem, which we did by around 1700 hours. Dark and cold was well and truly upon us when we arrived at our safe house for a few hours RandR which was food and sleep. Waking me at 2100 hours for the final leg, I had another hot drink and off we went around the back streets of Udem then breaking out into the woods again, twenty minutes or so and the familiar vertical finger across the mouth meant we were about to cross enemy lines for the third time got me thinking of how many times our luck would hold out.

We criss-crossed the woods as close to Gerry as before until about thirty minutes later a thumb up indicated we'd made it through. Although we were in occupied territory the feeling was a tad more relaxed and it stayed like that until we came to a hamlet apparently on the outskirts of Xanten where my safe house was.

In about twenty-eight hours I'd done thirty miles, crossed a river and three enemy lines but I'd made it!

The house was occupied by a young Dutch couple who were incredibly brave for putting me up, my "room" was in the attic but the hatch into it was cleverly hidden in the ceiling part of a wardrobe, it had no window as such just an open slit in the brickwork (which I guess was for ventilation) from which I could see the road below as well as the Rhine. The chimney breast going up through the attic gave me adequate warmth, my toilet was a bucket emptied daily by a hoist.

The Rhine was only a few hundred yards from my attic which gave me an amazing vista of road and river traffic. Across the river and a mile or so inland was the town of Wesel, apparently a Nazis communication centre and I'm guessing part of the reason B.S wanted me reporting back on traffic from this location and that became more evident by B.S almost daily request for up-dates of movements etc.

The giveaway there was to be a crossing at some point around here was their request for accurate river widths and locations of gradual sloping banks on either side and this meant a recce along the river bank each night to gather up info, of particular interest to B.S was the make-up of the banks, gravel or mud, firm or soft, clearly a detailed picture of the terrain was being created. Come the 17th or 18th (March) most of the Germans around here had retreated back across the Rhine and Wesel had become a frequent target for the air force, then a few days later I had confirmation from B.S *crossing 23rd-r v 46commando at ****on ******. So, this was it, the final push into Germany was about to begin.

Chapter Sixteen

Germany!

I think it was the night of the 22nd when I made the R.V with an advance troop of 46 Commando and although most of where we were had been cleared of enemy, we were still vulnerable to sniper and occasional artillery fire from across the river, so it was very much a silent operation as we made our way along the river bank several hundred yards downstream, to the point I thought most suitable to drop in the Buffaloes (motorised floating troop vehicles).

Silently the handful of marines scoured the opposite bank until as mad as ever someone said off you go lads, unbelievably three of them slid into the freezing river and swam to the other side a couple of hundred yards away. We saw them get out and disappear into the undergrowth, re-appearing some twenty minutes later to swim back over! Job done. Arriving back at the jeeps the first of an almighty air assault began on Wesel, bang after bang after bang, relentless and so accurate too, and I remember thinking there can't be anything (or anyone) left there! 46 made off and I returned to my base, thankfully we deemed it safe enough for me to vacate the attic and use the house now.

Next morning's W/T was to R.V. with 46 at the same spot at 1900 hours, which I did. They were all in good spirits and accepted me well knowing I'd completed all the training they'd been through had installed much mutual respect. Right on drop off time half a dozen Buffaloes arrived and 46 loaded while at the same time several R.A.F Typhoons swept in and beat up the area opposite, even so there was still sporadic fire coming from Nazi diehards. I watched the Buffaloes rise up and out the other side, drop off their load and return for the next for the next crossing, further upstream more marines were crossing in open boats. The Buffaloes loaded up again and were off and I said to the load master, "My turn next?"

"What? In civvies with no helmet?"

"S.O.E."

"Okay, next Buff then but get a bloody helmet!"

I tagged on with 45 Commando and blagged a helmet off a crew member, the crossing was only three or four minutes during which time I watched the RAF make run after run. Once over we broke out pretty rapid with news 46 Commando were well on their way to Wesel. Understandably I suppose some of the marines were reluctant to share their jeeps (and lives) with an unknown, so it took me several attempts before one marine offered me a ride, even so we didn't get far. The road was full of debris as well as a significant amount of bomb damage. Making our way on foot we were still coming under a considerable amount of fire, but slowly and surely, we made progress, silencing the enemy and taking about fifty POWs on the way, eventually getting into what was left of the town in the early hours.

By daylight the commandos had secured most of Wesel then a massive airborne drop took place to reinforce us. Now it was time for me to get on with my job which was to systematically go through as much as I could in the Nazis Communication centre (which despite the RAF wasn't completely flattened) looking for anything that may be of importance.

Personnel records, code books, frequency lists, orders from Berlin etc and although there was still much "stuff" there the Nazis burned most of what they couldn't take with them. I stayed around Wezel until the first week in April when I received a W/T to make for Manheim and meet up with an intelligence unit of the U.S army.

Managing to "claim" an abandoned German Jeep for the trip and given the Nazis were being pushed back at speed my journey there was uneventful until I reached the outskirts of the town and got stopped at a U.S check point. "Papers." Trying to explain my situation I could see I wasn't very convincing, "So you speak very good English? But you have French papers and a French I.D? No uniform or tag and in a German jeep? step out of the vehicle." So now I was banged up in a makeshift cell where I stayed for the rest of the day until the unit in town confirmed my authenticity!

Eventually getting released and having an escort to where I was to be based in a hotel on the outskirts of town I met with my American counterparts. Our brief the same, find anything that might be of importance, but then news came the British had just liberated Belsen concentration camp so we were particularly looking for anything that may be related to that, transport lists, orders given and received, anything that might be of use to the courts. During my W/T to B.S on the eighteenth I was tasked to go with the same U.S unit to a recently liberated Nazi labour camp and help with processing the interns.

Thankfully it was not a concentration camp in the true sense, these poor souls, mostly Jews had been held there as hostages. Relatives and often children of factory owners, industrialists, scientists and the like who were vitally important to the Nazis war machine and so to ensure their contribution to the war effort wouldn't be compromised the Nazis took their relatives — allowing them to write home once a month to confirm their existence, never the less it was not a pleasant experience, most of them had been worked very hard making munitions or loading magazines etc and on little more than starvation diets.

In all there were about twelve hundred there, mostly Dutch and Belgium's and our priority was food, medication, clothing and catalogue with statements. The adults were free to go (with a rail card and some dollars) but the younger ones were taken to reception centre where attempts were made to reconnect them with their families.

It was the first week in May and I received the numbing news on what was to be my last W/T — *stand down-* "Stand down? What? Do they think I'm a switch to be turned off after five years of pitting my wits against the Nazis, the Vichy, Franco's lot, the Malice?" I was so furious I just switched off without using any of my sign off codes or miss spelt words, my war was over. Now what?

Chapter Seventeen

819? The Hunt Begins

Now what indeed. Well, I still had a wad of dollars and although war was nearing the end and B.S. seemed to have no further use for me, I decided to go to Cologne and see the twin spires of the Cathedral (if it was still standing) before making my way to the channel and a ship home. Cologne was a mess but I could see most of the two spires were still in place. Once there I made contact with another U.S intel unit, while not telling them I'd been stood down they were very accommodating, feeding and watering me well, but after a few days there I decided it was time to make for home and my US hosts arranged for me to travel up to Nijmegen in one of their supply convoys, from there I could pick up the British going to and fro from Berlin. Nijmegen was also a mess especially the area around the bridge, I didn't know why but the number 819 came to mind and I began thinking about that dreadful event in the Dutch village which coincidentally must have been near here. Curiosity got the better of me and I decided to try and find that house — if only to see how that poor chap was, but for the life of me I couldn't remember the name of the village? Thinking an atrocity like that would not have gone un-noticed I decided to ask around the civilians here, one elderly man said the tragedy was much spoken about because it was at the home of a well-known and well-respected industrialist, he thought it was at a village called Melderslo, south of Venray, "How far is it and how do I get there?"

"It's about forty kilometres, take the bus to Venray then another to Melderslo, you can be there in under two hours."

Thanking him I asked, "Is there a small hotel near?"

"No, all destroyed, but you will be welcome to stay in my home tonight," and I did.

Next morning arriving in Venray, then changing to Melderslo, I still wasn't sure if this was the right thing to do and as we arrived at the outskirts of the village, I asked the driver to stop to let me off.

"Are you sure?"

"Yes, drop me off here and I'll walk the rest of the way — good bye!" Walking into the village brought back all the memories of that dreadful day and reaching the house (which I didn't realise was so grand) I wasn't sure if I even had the courage to knock, but I did. It was opened by an extremely thin, grey complexioned man probably in his mid-twenties. Nervously I asked if the gentleman who lived here was available, "That would be my father, why do you ask?"

As compassionately as I could I recalled to him how I arrived at the scene just as the Nazis were leaving and how I sat with his father that night. He shook my hand and gestured me in to the very same room only to see his father sat in the very same chair.

He recognised me in an instant and just sobbed and sobbed, it was so sad. Eventually he composed himself enough to get up, shake my hand and hug me like an old friend. Then the three of us went into another room, like a library where we sat around a huge table while the son, Levi, talked about events there. It transpired that the family were Jewish and owned a huge steel works near Eindoven. The Nazis ordered the father to produce ammo box's, fuel tanks, helmets etc, mostly using slave labour, but to make sure he didn't sabotage anything or slack in production they took him (Levi) to a labour camp in Dachau where he was held hostage for four years, the camp was liberated by the U.S and he arrived back home a week ago expecting to find his family in tact! Levi wanted to know more about the perpetrators who murdered his mother and sister, I told him how I had been subconsciously tracking the tank 819 ever since they committed genocide at Oradour-sur-Glane and then killed Raphael.

Never did I expect to run into them again, but I wondered how many other innocent souls that tank crew murdered. Then the father (Michael) turned to me and uttered, "Hunt them down. Hunt them down, please."

"But the war is over now and I'm on my way back to England."

"I will pay you."

"But I wouldn't know where to start, over half a million have been taken prisoner between here and Berlin alone."

"You will know how to hunt them down, I know you can do this for my family."

Levi went out of the room for a moment and returned with a wad of notes, "Here is one thousand dollars. Take this as your expenses for now, we are a very wealthy family, you can name your price, each one must pay for what they've done."

"I'm not sure I can do this, if I get caught, it would be murder."

"You won't get caught, you wouldn't have got through five years of war otherwise — we will pay you two thousand dollars for each and four thousand for the commander, that's twelve thousand dollars cash."

"Let me sleep on this please?"

"Okay."

Next morning at breakfast they asked for my decision, I replied, "The hunt is on!"

Chapter Eighteen

Berlin — Retribution Begins

Michael asked me how would I go about hunting these murderers down. My reply was simple, "I don't know." In my mind I'd already decided to begin at the end, Berlin — and early the next morning Levi drove me back to Nijmegen where I knew I could hitch a lift there, and I did in an empty field ambulance. It was late August and three months since the surrender had been signed. Germany had been divided into four sectors, British to the north incorporating much of Poland, the low countries to the west came under the French, to the south was the U.S and the east was Russian. Berlin was also to be included in the Russian annex. We were stopped at the Helmstedt checkpoint, which was pretty straightforward, then travelled a short distance to a field hospital where my I parted company with my lift.

Walking towards the centre of the city was surreal to say the least. Clearly it was becoming very much a Russian controlled city with Red Army guards at all the strategic points. The civilians were doing their best to pick up the pieces despite all around being just piles and piles of rubble where once fine buildings stood. Curiously, in among this were thousands of Allied troops wandering around sightseeing, I suppose they'd got to Germany and wanted to see for themselves the final destination before going home?

By late afternoon I was still making toward the centre of

Berlin and thoughts of 'Where do I spend the night and get some much-needed food' were uppermost when the most unexpected happened. Fate? Coincidence? Divine Intervention even?

"Seb — Seb is that you?" Turning around I was amazed to see my old school chum Walter Gibson! "Gibbo, you old devil! What in God's name are you doing here?" A joyous reunion was followed by much inquisitive chatter which transpired into Gibbo saying he was working for "the government" and had an office here which also doubled as his accommodation. "Where are you staying, Seb?"

"I have no idea."

"Well, you can stay with me, it's a bit damaged, but watertight!"

We continued walking a couple more streets until we came to Gibbo's building, obvious by the huge Union Jack draped form a top window. Clearly It once was a fine building but now had some serious damage, going up the steps and through the double doors I was amazed to find a well-equipped, fully functional office with a dozen or so typists all banging away at their machines and asking what they were all working away at Gibbo's reply was potentially music to my ears. "We're indexing and filing German POWs, a who's who of who did what etc, but primarily looking for the protagonists of the Nazis regime and war criminals too!"

"Blimey, Walter that must be one heck of a job."

"Yes, we've been at it for two months now and have so far catalogued over 400,000 POWs."

"So, Seb, tell me what you've been up to these past six years and what brings you to Berlin?" Tricky moment, but knowing I can trust my old school friend I decided to tell him some of what I'd been doing which included being with S.O.E, but I wasn't sure how to broach the subject of why I was in Berlin.

"Have you come across many war criminals yet?" I asked.

"Oh a few for sure, murderous bastards, they'll get their just desserts at the Nuremburg trials."

"But what about the ones who slip through the net Walter, how to they ever get dealt with?"

"No doubt some are being tracked down right now — paid for by the lucky ones."

"Mercenaries, you mean, Walter?"

"Yes, Seb and who's paying you and why?"

That direct question stumped me because I'd never thought of it like that, but he was quite right. "Good guess, Walter, have you heard of the mass murder carried out by the 2nd SS Panzers at Oradour-sur-Glane, Western France?"

"Yes, I have heard of that, Seb."

"I was S.O.E working with the local resistance, suffice to say we were first in there, my closest friend was cut down that day and more by accident I've been tracking the perpetrator all the way to Germany, he also committed another atrocity in Holland a month before the surrender."

"Can you identify him, Seb?" Walter asked.

"All I have is he was 2nd SS Panzer group, his tank was a Mk V Panther number 819 and he had a skull and cross bone painted on it, can you help me track him down, Walter, please?"

"Seb, I can get into serious trouble if I do."

"No one will ever find out Walter, you have my word on that my friend."

"Leave it with me for a day or two, meanwhile stay here with me and enjoy what's left of Berlin."

Dinner came via a chuck wagon as did breakfast too, nothing elaborate but it was perfectly edible. The day was spent wandering the streets again while mindful of Gibbo's advice not to go any further eastward. That evening I met with Gibbo in his office where he took delight in telling how he's got his best girl on the case and that he has good connections with other intelligence agencies, then came dinner, then came bed.

Breakfast next morning was interrupted by a knock at the door. "Mr Gibson."

"Yes, Alison."

"I have something here, that Panzer tank you're looking for. It was surrendered near Cologne."

"Excellent work Alison. Who to?"

"Looks likely to be the Durham's, but I'm still working on it."

"Well done, Alison let me know as soon as you have anything else."

"Clear off then, Seb and let us get on with our work," and so another day was spent roaming the streets, but this time with much anticipation after Alison's news.

It was late afternoon in Walter's office when a beaming Alison knocked and entered, "Think I've cracked it, sir."

"Go on, Alison."

"They surrendered on May 10th, the driver was Erhard **** but he was shot and killed while trying to escape, the radio operator/machine gunner is Kasper *** I have his address, it's a suburb in the eastern side of Berlin, the Loader is Dieter **** and he is from Cologne, the Gunner is Gunther **** from Siegen which is near Cologne and the commander is Baron Albert **** from near Munich. All are expected to be at the addresses given except the commander who was requested by the Americans to be handed over on war crime issues, which we did but they say an administration error led to him being released again, but I'm not so sure it was an error, more a deal?"

"Brilliant work, Alison, thank you very much." Alison left the room and Gibbo turned and said, "I suppose you have a job, or four to do now then, Seb?"

"Indeed, I do, Walter, my dear friend, indeed I do, I'm thinking Kasper in the east of the city first then to Cologne, next to near-by Siegen?"

"No," Walter replied, "Go to Cologne first while I make enquiries about Kasper, he's in Russian territory and that could be out of the question for you?"

"Okay, Walter, I'll be guided by you."

"We have a daily post run to Cologne (and back) it leaves each morning at 0800 sharp, be ready." I was.

Cologne was still a mess but becoming more orderly and thankfully the U.S guys I made contact with a few weeks previously were still there and just as accommodating. By now all of the concentration camps had been liberated and the horrors of the Nazi regime was coming to light which in turn created much bitterness, hatred even and as Walter had suggested there were "hunters" out there after revenge of which I believe to a certain extent the Allies were turning a blind eye to, indeed when my hosts asked me what brought me back to Cologne and I told them I was looking for two individuals they first asked if I was on official business? I paused the conversation, they then asked how they could help?

"Are Dieter **** and Gunther **** on your radar?" I asked.

"We'll take a look but it will take a few hours to check them out," again they asked if I was on official business and again I paused the conversation which eventually brought an, "Okay — go walk-about for a couple of hours and let's see what we can come up with."

As instructed, I returned later in the day to, "We got your two Seb, their names were given up by a Baron Albert ****, we requested your guys handed him to us as a war crime suspect and during his "interview" he revealed the names of his tank crew, lets pay them both a visit tonight." Without going into details, we did just that, suffice to say the following afternoon I was in the post van en-route back to Berlin — job done!

Think I took Walter by surprise when I walked into his office late in that afternoon. "Good god, man! What are you doing back here so soon? On second thoughts I don't want to know."

"Probably best you don't, Walter, have you made any progress in finding Kasper yet?"

"Yes, I have but I need to make a quick call, can you leave the room please?"

"Okay," then a few minutes later came the shout from Walter in his office, "Seb! Lord knows why I'm helping you with this so pay attention, tomorrow at 0700 hours I will accompany you to a junction not far from here where a car will be waiting to take you to another location, ask no questions of any one, if you mess up you may not come back, and worse still, I will lose my pension, understand?"

"Totally, Walter. Totally."

We met up around 0645 and walked about fifteen minutes to a car I guessed by the Russian pennant on the wing was for me, as we approached one man got out and holding the door open gestured me in. "Don't, for God's sake mess this up, Seb," said a worried looking Walter.

"Have faith, Walter, have faith," and off we drove.

No idea whose car I was in but it was noticeable that Red Army personnel often saluted or stood to attention as we passed, very impressive. We drove on for another ten or fifteen minutes, eventually pulling up outside what was once a huge building, but somewhat of a mess now. My chaperone (Rusky) jumped out and opened my door gesturing me to follow him, which of course I did. Up the steps and into a busy entrance hall while slowing to take in the ornate surroundings Rusky uttered, "Come, come," up the stairs to a pair of carved doors, a knock was met with something Russian from within. As Rusky opened the doors a very well-dressed man in perfect Queens English asked, "Ah you must be Mr Wyke?"

"Indeed, I am sir and who am I speaking with?"

"Oh, my name is of no importance to you, have you had breakfast?"

"Er, no," a brief exchange between Rusky and my host in their mother tongue took place and Rusky left the room. We moved over to a large dining table to one side of the room and sat at opposites to each other.

"So you have interest in the man Kasper, Mr Wyke?"

"Yes, I do."

"I Understand he's a war crime perpetrator"

"Yes, he certainly is."

"Are you one hundred percent positive?"

"I am." Then the conversation was paused as breakfast arrived, boiled eggs, bread, with a pot of tea. "Tell me please how and where did you learn to speak English so eloquently?"

"My father was Military Attaché to your country, we lived in London for almost ten years until he was recalled when war broke out, I miss your capital and its summer events, Ascot, Henley, Trooping the colour, we attended them all you know." Breakfast finished and cleared he asked what I intended to do with the man Kasper if ever I came across him and, deciding to be honest, I replied rather tongue in cheek, "Well I've not come here to invite him to Ascot."

That brought a smile of approval from my host who then pondered for a moment twiddling his thumbs until he looked up, "Okay, Mr Wyke — follow me."

Out of his office back down the stairs to the ground floor with Rusky on my heels, then to one corner where we went down a further set of stairs. Stopping at the bottom he said, "We chose this building because it was the former Gestapo HQ," and gesturing to the guard to open the heavy steel door he stood in front of I could see what he meant. We were in the basement of not a nice place, row upon row of small prison cells, probably twenty or so each side with two guards at the far end. "Are you one hundred percent about the man, Kasper?" he asked again.

"I am." He began walking into the vaulted cellar come prison come torture chamber, some cells were occupied, most not so, I couldn't help notice some of the walls had blood on them, this was an evil place for sure. Following, not knowing what to expect next, he stopped at a cell and called the guards who then came and un-locked the door. He spoke to the inmate in German but I caught word of him stating Kasper **** 2nd panzer and that was replied by a grunt of acceptance from the prisoner. At this point I had not set eyes on Kasper until I was gestured into the cell.

"This is the man, Kasper, what do you have to say to him?"

"Oradour-Sur-Glane." Kasper visibly shook, my host spoke to Rusky and then walked back to the entrance door, Rusky pulled a very small hand gun from the inside of his jacket the likes of which I'd not seen before, he attached a silencer and presented the weapon to me butt first. I turned and faced Kasper who by now knew what was about to happen and shook even more. I took aim at his forehead and pulled the trigger — he fell — job done.

I handed the weapon back to Rusky and walked away to find my host, with Rusky following. Up the stairs to the ground floor where my host was waiting.

"Good day to you, Mr Wyke, and give my regards to Walter," before I had the chance to reply he was off back up the stairs to his office. Rusky tapped me gently on the shoulder and pointed to the main door. Back in the car, past the Brandenburg gate to the location I was picked up at some four hours earlier. Walking back to Walters, I could see him waiting nervously outside.

"I am pleased to see you back."

"Thanks Walter, your Russian friend sends his best regards, three down, one to go, eh?"

Chapter Nineteen

The Baron

"Seb, I've been giving this a good deal of thought and I'm afraid I cannot allow you to go ahead with this."

"Why on earth not, Walter? The man's a murdering bastard!"

"Oh, no doubt Sebastian, problem being his family are a highly regarded part of the German Aristocracy and have been so for centuries and there's big difference between bumping of a couple of soldiers and a member of the countries elite, not only that he's living in the U.S. sector and the Yanks won't appreciate you being active under their noses, also to is the fact they once had him in their custody, but for reason known only to them they released him, he may have spilled the beans to them and given them valuable information?"

"So are you telling me Walter we have to turn a blind eye to him, let him get away with torching six hundred women and children?"

"Not at all, Seb, might I suggest a compromise? Go to his house in Munich, but with one of our German speaking officers and a Red Cap (military police) arrest him and take him to Nuremberg where he will be charged with war crimes, okay?"

"I won't go against your advice Walter and I'm drawing some satisfaction knowing there is enough evidence to find him guilty from which the bastard will be hung!"

"Good man, Seb, first thing in the morning be off then."

0600 hours and I met with Peter the officer, a guardsman and a proper chap he was too and the M.P. who was also an "upright" solid type. Walter insisted we wore civvies and used a car rather anything military looking, the logic was not to draw attention to ourselves by the Yanks.

It was a long drive down to Munich, almost six hours before we arrived at the village just south of the city where he apparently lives in some grandeur, and did he ever. A castle like building straight out of a nursery rhyme, with high almost mountainous rocks all around apart from a bridge over a deep ravine being the only entrance. As we drove up there was an elderly chap, a caretaker I reckon, doing some work on a wall and I suggested to Peter, "In your best German accent ask him if Baron Albert is at home." What was forthcoming was unbelievable to say the least!

"No, you missed him by a week."

"Really, where's he gone then?"

"To join his parents along with their loot."

"Sorry I don't understand, what do you mean?"

"Argentina — that's where they'll be."

"Don't be ridiculous, that's impossible and what loot?"

"The stuff they stole from the Jews, paintings, sculptures, gold, furniture — Loot!"

Clearly this old man was very bitter. "How on earth did they get that out of the country when there was a war on and how could they have escaped, how do we know he's not in hiding in the house?"

"I'll show you — follow me."

Once inside it was evident much of the pictures that had hung there had been taken down and there were obvious spaces where furniture and the likes had once been.

Peter suggested the chap came clean as to how and when the

place had been stripped and how the Baron's family left under the noses of the Allies?

"Money — Baron Frederic, Albert's father was one of the richest men in Germany, he was never in the military but moved in the highest Nazis circles, the Fuhrer even visited here."

"So how did he come by all the loot, as you put it?"
"He was financing the Nazis party and in exchange they gave him priceless works of art they took from the Jews."

"But how could they have possibly had this "Loot" taken all the way to Argentina during a world war? Quite impossible!"

"No, it went just before war was declared, in August '39, I crated it all up and packed all the silverware as well, took me nearly a week to pack and label it then I went in the lorry to the docks and loaded it onto a ship."

"Um — I'm not convinced, can you remember the name of the ship and what cargo line it was from and where were the labels addressed to?"

"Oh, it wasn't a cargo ship, it was a huge battleship, the Graf Spee out of Wilhelmshaven and I remember the destination as being Bariloche, Argentina." Peter was taken aback by this, everyone had heard of the Battle of the River Plate and how the Royal Navy had chased the Graf Spee into port only to be scuttled a few days later. There was huge speculation as to why a German capitol ship was thousands of miles away in the South Atlantic when war broke out, and now we may have been on the verge of discovering why. Removing millions of pounds worth of Jewish belongings to where they believed would be a safe haven.

Peter looked at me and asked if Walter was ever going to believe this.

"So where are Frederic and Albert now?" Peter asked.

"Frederic and the lady left here in September last year when it looked likely we were going to lose the war."

"But how the hell did they escape from occupied Europe, it was a veritable fortress then."

"The Vatican route."

"What — what on earth?"

"I expect by now you have found out the Vatican were long-time Nazi sympathisers, there is a monastery just over the border in Austria where the Archbishop, a man called Alois Hudal, will provide Nazis with papers and a safe passage via other monasteries over the Alps to Rome, then further south where they catch a ship to Syria, then it's easy to cross Africa to get another ship to South America."

"Are you telling the truth, you will be in serious trouble if you're hiding Albert here or hindering His majesty's Government."

"It is truth, I swear, Albert left here last week to go the same route, I drove him there, I can take you across the border now and show you the monastery, it is only forty-five minutes away."

"Okay," Peter replied, "Let's go."

With the four of us in the car and following our guides directions we crossed into Austria seemingly without a checkpoint, shortly after we arrived at a monastery. "This is it, this is where I dropped Albert off last week and his parents last year."

"I can't believe all this," Peter said, "It just seems impossible, I want to go back to the house and do a more thorough search of the place."

So we did just that and our search found absolutely nothing except for one important find, a photograph of Baron Albert on his Panther V tank number 819, proof if ever I needed it.

Back in Berlin we sat for an hour or more with Walter

explaining and revealing what we'd apparently discovered which in short was a Vatican organised and funded Nazis escape route all the way to South America. However, much to mine and Peters astonishment Walter appeared unimpressed, dismissive almost until Peter suggested this may not have been so much of a secret to the Allies, after all at which point Walter insisted we drop the subject and go for dinner, but Peter was insistent, "What do you know, Walter, what's going on here?"

Walter spoke, "This goes no further than these four walls, Okay? It's long been suspected-"

"You mean known," interrupted Peter.

"The Vatican was known to be sympathetic to the Nazi's Anti-Semitism program even to the point where evidence suggests some priests were Nazi collaborators, but for fear of upsetting our new Italian Allies it was decided on high to keep the lid on this, but now war is over it may be progress will be made into just how much the Vatican was involved."

"Seb, you've lost your man, now can we change the subject and go for dinner please?"

Dinner was a fairly subdued affair, apart from being very tired both Peter and myself were somewhat disillusioned by the fact that politics had taken the precedence over people. Next morning and with no reason to stay in Berlin a moment longer I said farewell to my dear friend Walter, he could see I wasn't happy with how things transpired and politely asked, "Where now?"

"Oh, back to blighty and farming I guess, Gibbo, maybe call in on the Dutch family en-route."

"Well look after yourself and be sure to keep in touch, old boy," as he handed me his contact details.

"Cheerio then Walter and thanks for all your help."

Chapter Twenty

The Biggest Decision

With another lift to Nijmegen then a bus to Michael's house, it was Levi who answered my knock on the door.

"Come in, Seb, good to see you again and to be honest both my father and myself didn't think you would ever return."

"Well, I'm here and with much to tell." With that Michael appeared (not looking good either) and after a few words of welcome he asked if I'd made any progress hunting down his family's murderers and without revealing too much detail, especially about those who collaborated with me I told them what I'd achieved. "I managed to identify and track down the five-man crew of the tank 819, they were captured prior to the end of the war, the driver was Erhard ****, he was shot while trying to escape. The loader was Dieter **** and the gunner was Gunther ****, I dispatched both, the machine gunner was Kasper ****, I shot him in Berlin, but disappointingly the commander, Baron Albert **** escaped."

"We knew you could do this for us, Sebastian," said a very tearful Michael, "But the man Albert? I don't understand, how did he escape and where is he now, I don't understand that."

"Well, Michael, I still find it hard to believe but I have strong evidence to suggest he escaped to South America."

"How was that possible, he's a war criminal!"

"Yes, I agree but evidence I've uncovered implicates the Vatican sponsoring an escape route for the Nazis from a monastery in Austria, then into Italy, then via several routes to South America," with that Levi spoke.

"There were rumours of this happening when I was in Dachau, some of the inmates there, especially from Italy and Serbia spoke of this, some priests were Nazi collaborators."

"Exactly, Levi, exactly."

"Then he must be tracked down, Sebastian, he cannot be allowed to get away, he must pay for his wicked ways," said Michael.

"I agree with you, Michael, but there is no extradition agreement with South American countries so there is no way of getting him back and that's providing we could even find him."

"Then for the sake of my family and my people, Sebastian. I beg you, go to South America, find him and do what you must to make him pay!"

"Michael, that would be almost impossible, to get into a country on a different continent in a different hemisphere with no papers, track down someone who's in hiding, deliver justice, then return somehow, it's a nonstarter."

"Have you an idea which country he is in," asked Michael.

"Yes, Argentina, he arrived in Buenos Aires, but moved on from there."

With that Michael stood up, "We can get you there, Sebastian, yes we can do that."

"How on earth do you propose to do that, Michael?"

"Before war we had two freighter ships taking coal to Buenos Aries in exchange for Iron Ore, they have no coal and we no Ore. They leave on the first day of each month, one come, one goes, in war they operated from Barcelona and the ore was brought up from Spain by rail, but we have now begun operations once more from Rotterdam, we can get you there and back on our ships and our port agent in B.A is also Jewish, he will help too, you have to do this for us please, Sebastian!"

Levi left the room for a moment and returned with a money bag, here, "Here is your payment for work you have done so far and another four thousand for your expenses in South America, take it, please?"

"Hold on a moment, I need to think about this for a while, of course Sebastian, our ship the Jeremiah leaves Rotterdam on November 1st, ten days' time."

We had dinner together that evening and as much as my serious head was telling me to turn down their offer, my stupid head was thinking of the adventure, sleep didn't much happen that night.

We had breakfast together and Levi asked if I'd thought any more about their proposal. "I've had little else on my mind Levi, is your telephone capable of connecting to England, I've not spoke with my parents for almost eighteen months."

"Yes, it should do that, if you have some patience," he replied.

"Good, can I make a call please?"

"Of course, we will leave you alone now, we have a factory to run and you have nine days to decide."

"Mother, is that you?"

"Sebastian, oh my Sebastian, where have you been all these months, we thought you were dead, where are you now why didn't you contact us?" Mother was so emotional and I felt so guilty.

"Mother it has been a long journey for me, but war is over and I should be with you in a week or two, how is everyone?"

Mother went on to say all was good at Windy Ridge but that her family in France have not had such a good time, the Germans took all their animals, Cattle and Sheep to feed their army and a year ago two stray bombs from an allied plane had hit their milking parlour and main barn flattening both, they'd had no income for two years and had no money to buy new stock or re-build their barns.

"I'm so sorry to hear that, Mother, perhaps when I return, I can take you to visit them?" Mother agreed, we said our good byes (again) and ended the call with a 'see you soon'.

Thoughts of my grandparents struggling troubled me, to the point where I asked Levi if he had a car I could use for a few days to visit my family in France. "Yes, of course, you can take mine."

"Thank you, Levi, can I take one thousand dollars too?"

"Of course."

Early next morning I was off to Western France, a journey I reckoned I could just about do in a day, in fact it was dark by the time I arrived at the farm.

The welcome my Grandparents (and uncle and aunt too) gave me was a very emotional affair for all of us and the strain of living in an occupied country had taken its toll on all of them, especially my grandparents. We had a meal and chatted well into the night mostly about the occupation and their hardship, then when I produced the dollars that brought even more tears!

In the morning they gave me a tour of the damaged out-buildings including a small barn my cousin Philip was using as a garage come repair shop, it was then I had an idea. "I need to take you for a twenty-minute drive, ready?" With cousin Philip and my grandparents on board we set off, "Where are we going, Sebastian?" they asked.

"Well, I know where we're going but not sure what we will find there, so be patient for a little while longer." Coming to a fork in the road I could see it, Raphael's garage and home, I pulled onto the forecourt to see that apart from a few tiles missing it was in pretty good shape, come on then. Philip new the place, "This was the home of Raphael, the resistance fighter he was killed last year, very brave man." It was Philip and with the door key I'd kept in my pocket as a memento of my time with me dear friend I opened the door, "Why have you got a key, how do you know this place?" asked a very inquisitive Philip. Then my Grand Father said, "It is known that Raphael worked with a British Agent, is that you Sebastian?" I couldn't and didn't answer that. Once inside everything was just as I recalled, I knelt down at the range cooker and pulled out the bottom drawer, then with my hand inside as far as I could reach, I pulled the secret floor panel up and to my immense joy retrieved Raphael's leather pouch which I placed on the table asking Philip to open it, he did and pulled out a wad of French Francs along with the deeds to the building.

"Raphael was my dearest friend and he often said that with no family if anything ever happened to him, he wanted me to have this property, so now it's mine, so now I gift it to you Philip." More tears followed by more tears and many hugs too. Back at the farm we had a little lunch and with a promise of bringing my mother to see them as soon as we could make it, we said our farewells. Feeling pleased with myself and the good deeds done but also realising it was too late in the day to get back to Holland in one journey I decided to go via Orleans and look up Nadine, the lady who took me in a year ago.

Finding her house wasn't too much of a problem, but what happened next was. A knock at the door was answered by an elderly lady. "Hello, can I speak with Nadine please, she helped me last year?"

"Monsieur, you do not know?"

"Know what please?"

"Nadine is no longer with us, the Gestapo took her last July, they had a tip off she was sheltering a British agent, they interrogated her, beat her terribly, she did not tell anything so they took her to Ravensbruck concentration camp and murdered her." My body went cold, a freezing shiver the likes I've never experienced.

"I am so sorry, au-revoir." Back in the car I just broke down, why is it good things are always followed by bad, I don't think I have ever cried like that before, not even as a child and all the way back to Holland I thought of nothing else other than the time I spent with Nadine and how much she must have suffered at the hands of the Nazis — and most probably all of my doing too!

It was early morning when I arrived at my Dutch friend's house and Levi welcomed me. "Levi, I've decided, I will go to South America, but not until spring, I need to spend some time with my parents and to research more about Argentina. I will return in February for a March sailing, okay?"

"Excellent news, Seb, Father will be pleased, let me get you your money and gun," Levi returned with the money and my Webley that he'd kept for safe keeping, we said our good-byes and with my promise to return we shook hands — home here I come.

Chapter Twenty-One

To Argentina

Christmas '45 was a peculiar time for me in that although the war had been over for six months and try as I might to put the some of the horrendous events I'd witnessed out of my mind (Oradour-sur-Glane and finding Michael's wife and daughter, Nadine) I was being constantly reminded of them by more and more revelations of the Nazis "Final Solution". The atrocities, the camps, just awful times that was beginning to affect me. Sleep was a problem, but I also became aware of a creeping obsession to seek revenge/justice call it what you want and it made me even more determined to track down Baron Albert, wherever he was! Referring back to my Sandhurst days and the three key objectives — Identify = Yes, plan — not yet! Execute — not yet, so a plan needed to be hatched. I spent hours in our local library researching Argentina in particular where Bariloche was and how to get there from Buenos Aries and I concluded the twice weekly two-day coach journey was my best option even though it was a one-thousand-mile trip to the other side of Argentina. I also thought it good if I made contact with Levi's port agent before I arrive, so I wrote to Levi asking if he could forward address etc of his contact (which he did).

My dear friend Walter Gibson was in London for the festivities and I managed to get the train up and spend a day with him, but that unfortunately didn't end as I would have liked.

Walter asked what my plans were for the year ahead to which I replied I was contemplating going to Argentina to track down the Baron he broke into a veritable rage stating the idea was preposterous and that I would never come back! He went on to say he would wash his hands of me if I went through with it because of the diplomatic explosion that would follow if I were to get caught, stubbornly though, Gibbo's words fell on my deaf ears.

Early February and I broke the news to my parents that I needed to be away training some Canadians for about three months, that didn't go down well especially with Father who knew I was lying!

Arriving at the port office in Rotterdam on the last day of February I was greeted by Levi's master of the Jeremiah, a good sort who showed me to my bunk in the mess room then introduced me to some of the other crew on board as a new general hand for the journey to B.A. Next day we cast off and began our three-week journey south. Life on board was very routine, but ok, I got on well with the other crew who were mostly Dutch, however, the nearer we got to our destination the more my thoughts were on how I was going to do this, that's assuming I could even track him down.

I didn't dare bring my handgun, instead my knife and two L tabs (cyanide tablets) left over from my S.O.E days. Increasingly too Gibbo's remarks about not coming back echoed in my mind. Three weeks sped by, and we docked in B.A whereas promised Levi's agent was there to meet me. I had two enjoyable days staying with him and his family then with not very much by way of kit I boarded the bus to Bariloche, what a journey that was! We had an overnight stop in the back of beyond in some pit of a guest house finally arriving at Bariloche late evening. Thankfully my research came up with a small guest house where I'd made a booking for three weeks, (that was on the assumption I could do what I needed to do in that time) then get back to B.A. to catch the ship back to Holland?

My first full day there was such a revelation, judging by the similarity of the buildings and general architecture here you could be easily mistaken this town was not an Alpine one in Europe. Beautiful wooden lodges and chalets were mirror like of any Tyrolean town, but most amazing was the number of times I heard the German language being spoken, even more so was the often-seen Nazi flag being displayed in private houses. Clearly, I was not going to be inconspicuous here!

With just three weeks to find the Baron I decided to visit as many bars, cafes and restaurants as I could, but finding him was not going to be easy.

The centre of town around the lakeside seemed to be a popular place for the German's, especially the terraces where they would sit all day reminiscing, I guess, and unbelievably some of the bars even had photos on the walls of German military and Nazi hierarchy, a few of whom I recognised, it was hard to believe this was Argentina!

Several days passed with no luck at all although I'm convinced some of the German's I was seeing quite regularly were "notorious". But my luck took an amazing turn for the good when feeling peckish I went into a small bakery and joined the queue.

They were very busy when the young assistant shouted through to the back for help and although I was neither fluent in German or Argentinean/Spanish, I'd picked up enough on my travels to make out what she said, "Can you serve, Baron Frederic?" That's the name of Albert's father! Appetite gone I left the shop and waited across the road for Frederic — hoping to follow him home.

He wasn't aware of me shadowing him, a couple of lefts and rights and he arrived at what I presumed to be his home and that of Albert too. Sure enough, just a few minutes later Baron Albert appeared on the balcony, result! But now the hard bit, if I knifed or strangled him, I'd need to dispose of his body and that could be difficult, if I didn't and he was discovered then there would be a murder to investigate and probably the only Englishman in Bariloche would render me a prime suspect? Accident — possibly? L tabs (cyanide) — a good option as it would leave no marks and suggest a heart attack as the cause, but how to administer, how could I get close enough?

My plan was to shadow him for a few days to see where he eats/drinks and that soon showed he went to a bar each afternoon around four p.m. where he would stay until five-thirty then leave for home. If only I could get close enough to him. Next day I decided to be at the bar before him, sure enough four p.m. he arrived and sat at his usual table for two overlooking the lake, very routine. I did the same next day but decided to sit at his table, he arrived and walked over clutching his beer, he stood right by my side and said something in German. I replied no "Sprichst du Deutsch."

"Ah Englander, you are a long way from home, what brings you here?"

To which I replied, "That's a very long story," then getting up from my seat "I may tell you one day, goodbye."

So now I'd made contact, next was to win his confidence, then to execute! Next day I went back to the bar making sure I arrived before the target, sure enough at four p.m. he appeared and with beer in hand he sat down. "So tell me of your long story."

"Oh, it wouldn't be of interest to you, suffice to say England was my home, but stupidly greed clouded my judgement now I can never return."

"Tell me more please."

"Tomorrow perhaps, I have to go now, bye."

Next day at exactly the same the Baron joined me again and I have to say we were getting on quite well, if only he knew I was about to kill the murdering bastard.

"Tell me more of your long story."

"Okay, I was not long out of Oxford University and worked for Bletchley Park, the government communications HQ, all was good until one day I was approached by one of the professors from my old college suggesting how I could be paid handsomely for passing some simple bits of information, it seemed a harmless way of earning a lot of money, if only!

"First it was simple things like ship call signs, airfield I.D. then it got more specific."

"What like — what do you mean?" By then I was handling British agents and I gave the contact an awful lot of information — "who was the contact" — never knew his name, I would meet him each Saturday, I would pass him an envelope full of info and he would give me one full of money — "so why are you on the run from England" — a few weeks before war ended he was arrested, my old professor said he would spill the beans on me and if that happened I would be hung, hence I've gone as far from England as possible."

"So now you are more German than English. I will buy you a beer." He did, I drank it and with a "See you tomorrow," I left. Was my plan coming together? I think so, enough for me to consider the next day as his last.

Next day, same time same table and Albert appeared with

beer in hand as usual. There followed some small talk and he raised the subject of me being a spy again, "So what will you do now, what will you do for work?"

"It's my time to buy you a beer now, Albert," at the bar I ordered two more beers and while the bar tender wasn't looking, I slipped both L tabs into Albert's last drink. Taking the beers back to the table and praying I hadn't mixed the glasses up I knew I had to switch glasses the moment he succumbed, he took a big gulp of beer and immediately froze, his eyes protruded, then glazed then with his hand on his neck he choked and was gone! Before anything I had to switch glasses — done — then "accidentally" knock my new glass (with the tab in) over so as to destroy the evidence — done — Next call for help — Running into the bar shouting, "The Baron has had a heart attack, come quickly, quickly!" And it looked my plan had worked. A doctor arrived and pronounced him dead, cause, probable heart attack, job done!

My next step was to stay here for another four or five days so as not to raise suspicion by leaving immediately after his death, then catch the bus back to B.A. I continued to go the bar each day at four p.m. and even got to know the bar man who on my last day there I told it was time for me to continue my travels, explaining I was off to Chile next.

Arriving back in B.A on the last day of the month ready to leave on the ship in the morning I was horrified to find because of predicted bad weather the ship left thirty-six hours ago! So now I was stuck in B.A for another month and although Levi's friends offered to accommodate me at their house again the thought of staying there for that length of time, didn't please me much. However, I spent most of my time wandering around B.A and once more I was shocked at the number of Germans there were, and again I was sure I'd seen some of them in the newspapers as wanted war criminals, but that was not my problem any more. My hosts were excellent, and the time there soon passed.

The sailing back to Rotterdam was calm and uneventful, once docked my friend Levi greeted me with a simple question, "Yes, or no?"

"Yes, Levi, job done, how is your father?" Levi's eyes filled.

"Sadly, he died three weeks ago, they say of a heart attack but it was more of a broken heart."

"I am so sorry to learn that Levi and sorry that he passed before he knew how my task went."

"Oh, he knew, Seb — he told me he felt it." With that he passed me a small case, "Thank you, Seb, please keep in touch." We shook hands and that was the end of my quest.

Chapter Twenty-Two

Life As a Farmer?

Apart from the dressing down I had from Mother, my return to Windy Ridge was a much-welcomed chance to rest, recoup and reflect on the past seven years or so and to pick up on my life as a farmer (son) again. My dear friend Gibbo kept in regular touch and we would often meet up and reminisce about all sorts, school life, the war and my time in Argentina of which Walter, (who was still working in intelligence) always seemed particularly interested in. The 1940s drifted into the 1950s and all was going well until one dreadful day when one of the hands came running into the yard screaming in panic.

Father was mowing grass up on the Ridgeway when on a bad slope the tractor toppled over crushing him, he died instantly. It was horrendous for us all, especially Mother. His funeral was attended by many local dignitaries and most if not all the village lined to road to the church, such was his standing in the village and local community. By now it was around 1953 and mother, unsurprisingly said she wanted to go back to France to live with her now elderly parents and sister saying there was nothing left for her here anymore. A month or so later I accompanied Mother to her family in France, it was a reunion touched with happiness and much sadness, of course.

Over dinner one evening grandfather, a little worse for Calvados said to Mother, "Of course, Monique, you know

Sebastian is a hero here."

"What do you mean?" replied mother and Grandfather began to tell some of the exploits of Raphael the resistance fighter and his English accomplice going on to say how I visited them after the war (which mother knew nothing about) All very embarrassing.

Back at Windy Ridge, (which mother had signed over to me) life was going hard, the same thing every day with little time out for anything else, it got to a point when I'd had enough and after a brief discussion with mother seeking her consent I decided to sell up and move on, somewhere! Then I had a letter from Gibbo asking me to call him, which I did. He wanted me to meet two of his "international" colleagues but as much as I wanted to do that, I explained there was too much going on at the moment for me to get to London, "No problem," he replied, "We'll come to you," two day later he did.

Greeting Walter and his two friends with handshakes and exchange of names was a polite and gentlemanly affair, but once inside the conversation soon became extremely serious. Seated around the kitchen table, the conversation went something like this. Walter spoke first. "Seb, my two colleagues work for the Israeli intelligence agency, we met after the war while I was still in Germany and they were involved in the Nuremberg war crimes trials, now they're tasked primarily with tracking down Nazi war criminals."

"Do you mean Mossad?"

"Yes," one answered and went on to say. "Apparently, you had a "holiday" in Bariloche and know the area well?" With that I looked aghast at Walter, why would he divulge that to any one? Walter nodded reassuringly at me, "It's okay, Seb, you can trust these with your life." The other then said how they'd had an agent there for over a year looking for a specific person but drew a complete blank, he went on to say they had solid evidence he left Germany after the war via the Priest Line and was living in Argentina, then the bombshell came when he asked me if I would track the man down!

"Are you serious?" I looked across the table at Walter for guidance, but there was none forthcoming. "Who is this Nazis who's so important then?" With that he opened his case and produced two photographs, one of the men in Nazi uniform, the other in civilian clothing. "I recognise this man."

"You should, he was Adolf Hitler's right-hand man, he organised the building and running of the concentration camps, he has the blood of six million of our people on his hands, we don't speak or write of his name for fear of our mission becoming exposed, Argentina is a country of Nazi sympathisers, he is referred to only as 3, okay?"

"So what's your plan?" I asked.

"We want you to go to Bariloche, track him down, once that's been achieved, we have a plan to kidnap him and bring him to Israel for trial."

"When I said I recognised him I didn't just mean from his photographs, what's more you won't find him in Bariloche either because he's in B.A. When I missed my ship back, I had to spend another month there and most days I'd eat at a pavement cafe to the north of the city and he would walk past, presumably on his way home from work because he wore overalls."

"Are you sure, Seb? Are you 100% positive?" they both asked.

"Yes, I am."

"So, Sebastian will you go back to Argentina and help us bring him to Israel?"

Again, looking at Walter for guidance all he said was, "Your call, Seb — but if you're I.D. comes to light at all there will be no coming back to England." To which one of the Israelis countered I would be given full Israeli Nationality, "Our government and people would be eternally grateful to you, you would not go without I promise."

So, I was thinking with mother settled in France, the farm about to be sold and this adventure on the horizon, why not, why not indeed?

"Okay, I'm in, but I want to operate on my own until I find him, then I'm out."

"Excellent, Sebastian, excellent."

"But I will need a few months to get the farm sold then to make my way south."

"Yes of course Sebastian, your call on everything."

"Okay, I'll let Walter know when I'm on my way to B.A and we'll go from there?" My plan was to sail to B.A on my friend Levi's ship again and once there to see if his agent there would house me once more or at least recommend somewhere to stay for a while.

The sale of the farm dragged on and it was late 1959 before I was on my way to B.A. where on arrival Levi's agent met me and took me to his home. It was good to see them all again and how much his children had grown. Although we never spoke of my reason for being in Argentina again, I think he knew it wasn't for the climate and understandably he had arranged an apartment in town for me to use.

Back at the same cafe at the same time hoping and praying Walter's colleagues' faith in me wouldn't be wasted I was over the moon when on the second day the man, 3, walked past. Instantly I recognised him but playing safe I let him pass by deciding instead to try and shadow him, the next day, I picked him up at the end of the street and followed him for two blocks then turned away, the following day I picked him up again from where I left off the previous day, this I did for four days until I found where he lived and thinking all I have to do now is pass the location to Walter and catch the next ship home — such wishful thinking!

Walter came back requesting I meet with an Israeli agent who unbeknown to me was also in B.A. Reluctantly I agreed and a rendezvous was arranged for next day near the port. Needless to say, I was watching the meeting point two hours prior to the meet time and all seemed safe as far as I could ascertain and so a meeting of two spies from two countries came about with the sole intention of working together to kidnap a mass murderer and bring him to court.

There was not much by way of conversation other than was I a hundred percent certain the man I identified was the man known as 3. Yes, I was. "Good can you come to this address tomorrow at eleven a.m.?"

"Yes, good. See you tomorrow."

Next day at eleven a.m. I found the address to be a smallish hotel and going inside I could see it was being frequented by airline crew from various countries, the man I met the previous day greeted me and took me up to a room where once inside I was introduced to three other men there.

Pleasantries over, they thanked me for my work but then asked me to help them execute their kidnap plan, however I declined their request saying I only agreed to locate him, "That's what you're paying me for, no more." They were very insistent to the point where I agreed to review their plan.

"The evening before the scheduled El Al (Israeli Airlines)

flight out of B.A takes place we will bundle him into a car on his way home from work, we take him to a warehouse where he will be tranquilised, we will dress him in El Al flight uniform as we all will be. Next, we will drive to the airport and 3 will be bandaged so as to look like he's had a bad car crash, unconscious we will take him through customs and onto the aircraft and to Israel, what do you think?"

"In a word? Ridiculous, for a start I have no uniform?"

"We have one for you here."

"I have no papers, not even a passport?"

"Yes, you have, here is your Israeli passport and your boarding papers."

"If this comes off what happens when I get to Israel?"

"You will be a hero and our country will be your new home."

"I've never heard of such a fragile, full of risk plan in all my life!"

"But are you in? We desperately need you!"

"Reluctantly, yes, I'm in," and so a date for the operation was set for the following Friday evening. Thinking this might be my last adventure I wrote to Walter giving him an up-date and what to do with my belongings should I not return.

Friday came — four days later these were the international headlines:

The Israel Times:

Israel Announces Capture of Nazi War Criminal Adolf Eichmann

On May 23, 1960, the Israeli government reported the capture of Adolf Eichmann, the architect of the Holocaust, who had hidden for a decade in Argentina. Nazi SS officer Adolf Eichmann had orchestrated the roundups and transportation of Jews to Nazis concentration camps. After World War II ended, he managed to escape U.S custody and travel secretly out of Germany with the help of Nazi sympathizers. In 1950, using a fake passport and visa for "Ricardo Klement," he reached Argentina, where several other former Nazis had already settled.

The Mossad, Israel's Secret Service, acting with an unnamed agent pursued Eichmann and eventually tracked him to Buenos Aires. Acting without the permission of the Argentine government, (which did not allow other countries to extradite criminals), Agents secretly observed Eichmann before launching its plan to capture him.

On the evening May 11, 1960, the agents waited for Eichmann to come off a bus and walk home. the agents leapt out of a car at Eichmann, he was captured and taken to a safe house and secretly flown out of the country on an El Al plane on May 20.

On May 23, Israeli Prime Minister David Ben-Gurion

announced to the Israeli parliament, that Eichmann had been captured!

"I have to inform the Knesset that a short time ago one of the greatest of all Nazi war criminals, Adolf Eichmann, who was responsible, together with the Nazi leaders, for what they called 'the final solution' of the Jewish question, that is, the extermination of 6,000,000 of the Jews of Europe, was found by the Israeli Security Services and after executing a meticulously planned operation was brought to Israel where he will now stand trial for his crimes" he declared.

Adolf Eichmann was found guilty and sentenced to death by hanging.
Photo: credit YadVashem Holocaust Remembrance

> If anyone asks me, what do I do — my reply is quite simple:
> "Now I grow Oranges."

Nadine — S.O.E agent.

Lilian Verna Rolfe, born in Paris 1914 as one of a pair of twins to British parents who moved with her family from Paris to Rio in the 1930's. Fluent in French she made her way to England in 1943 to join the war effort where she volunteered to join S.O.E. Given the code name of Nadine (also Recluse and Claudine) she was landed in occupied France in April of 1944. Her work with the French resistance was vital, apart from an accomplished wireless operator she also accompanied the resistance in combat. Captured in July of that year she was brutally interrogated at Gestapo H.Q in Orleans then in August transferred to Ravensbruck concentration camp.

Implicated in a failed escape plan she was put to hard labor on a starvation diet. Close to death on the 5th of February she was carried from the punishment block to the cremation block and shot once in the back of her head.

Lilian Verna Rolfe, a.k.a. 9907 Nadine, is remembered on the Brookwood memorial, Runnymede, England.

Glossary

B.E.F, British Expeditionary Force.
B.P, Bletchley Park, top secret communications base.
B.S, Baker Street, the London Head Quarters of Special Operations Executive.
B.A, Buenos Aries, the capitol city of Argentina.
C.O, Commanding Officer.
Civvies, civilian clothing.
Djellaba, typical clothing worn by Berber's of North Africa.
D.L.I, The Durham Light Infantry.
Fairbairn, developed by Fairbairn and Sykes is a double edge fighting knife.
L Tab, cyanide tablet (suicide pill)
Malice, Vichy France collaborators and enemy of the allies.
Maquis, French resistance fighters on the side of the allies.
N.L.F, National Liberation Front, Algerian freedom fighters and later government.
O.T.C, Officer Training Corps.
Operation Torch, allied invasion of North Africa.
Operation Chariot, raid on the port of St Nazaire.
Operation Dynamo, the recovery of the B.E.F and allies from Dunkirk.
Operation Overlord, allied invasion of Normandy, June 6th 1944 (D-Day).
P.E, plastic explosives.
P.T.I, Parachute Training Instructor. suffix "I" with "S" for school.

Recce unit, Reconnoitre unit.
R.B.R, Royal Berkshire Regiment.
R.T.R, Royal Tank Regiment.
R.V, rendezvous.
Steno, Steganography, sending/receiving coded information via concealed micro dots.
S.O.E, Special Operations Executive.
W/O, Warrant Officer.
W/T, Wireless Transmission.
40, 45 etc, Commando Units.
30 A.U, 30 Assault Unit.